Allie pulled a pumpkin off the vine

"I'm choosing this one." Mike gazed at her. They were alone in the pumpkin patch. Allie looked into Mike's eyes, her pulse rate picking up frantically when she saw the desire in them.

"If you were a pumpkin," she said softly, "you'd be everyone's first choice. You have the height, the looks and the charm."

Mike took a step closer to her. His voice was low and seductive when he asked, "Charm's important in a pumpkin?"

Allie took a step toward him, too, so they were almost touching. "Nothing's more important than charm. In fact—"

His arms wrapped around her, pulling her close. A jolt of warning danced through her. She ignored it. She'd wanted this kiss for so long. So what if it wasn't smart? Who said she had to be smart all the time?

Dear Reader,

Surprises can be wonderful, but they can also change your life. For Mike Foster, one surprise turns his world upside down. Truthfully, he's not too happy about it. He has a good life, one he's built carefully over the years, and he doesn't want it to change.

But whether he likes it or not, Mike finds himself the guardian of his baby half brother. And Mike Foster never shirks his responsibilities. He accepts the challenge, and with the help of a special woman he soon discovers that while being a good dad may not be easy, it is definitely worth the effort.

We hope you enjoy Mike's story. We all get hit with surprises, and dealing with the good ones—and the bad ones—can sometimes be difficult. But as Mike finds out, the best approach is to square your shoulders and meet the challenge head on.

Besides, you never know when a surprise may turn out to be just what you need.

We love to hear from our readers. Feel free to drop us an e-mail at DalyThompson@aol.com.

Barbara and Liz

Surprise Dad
DALY THOMPSON

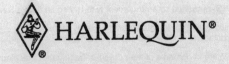

HARLEQUIN®

TORONTO • NEW YORK • LONDON
AMSTERDAM • PARIS • SYDNEY • HAMBURG
STOCKHOLM • ATHENS • TOKYO • MILAN • MADRID
PRAGUE • WARSAW • BUDAPEST • AUCKLAND

Recycling programs
for this product may
not exist in your area.

ISBN-13: 978-0-373-75301-7

SURPRISE DAD

Printed in U.S.A.

ABOUT THE AUTHOR

Daly Thompson is a collaboration between Liz Jarrett and Barbara Daly, both accomplished writers. Liz has been writing stories since she was a child. After graduating from college, she was a technical writer for twelve years before she decided to stay home with her children. During their naps, she started writing again, this time focusing on fiction. She naturally turned her attention to her favorite type of stories—romances.

Barbara brings to this joint effort her passion for reading, the characters she's collected from the diverse places she's lived and jobs she's held, and a strong preference for happy endings. She began writing when she discovered she needed a mobile career to match her husband's and at last found her own happy ending in writing romance.

Books by Daly Thompson

HARLEQUIN AMERICAN ROMANCE

Don't miss any of our special offers. Write to us at the following address for information on our newest releases.

Harlequin Reader Service
U.S.: 3010 Walden Ave., P.O. Box 1325, Buffalo, NY 14269
Canadian: P.O. Box 609, Fort Erie, Ont. L2A 5X3

To my mom and dad—
thank you so much for all the years of love and joy.
And to George—thanks for being a terrific surprise dad.

Chapter One

"Allie Hendricks is back in town."

Mike Foster, halfway through dialing his wholesaler to blast him for a late delivery, hung up the phone and stared at Barney, his short-order cook. "Allie? She can't be. It's the beginning of the semester."

"All I know is she's back."

"For the weekend, maybe?"

Barney skillfully flipped a few eggs. "Nope. She quit med school. Showed up last night and dropped the bomb on her mother. Elaine's having a fit."

Mike was stunned. "I can imagine."

"It's a real shame," Barney went on. "If anybody had the smarts to be a doctor, it was Allie. Just goes to show you. Can't figure out people no matter how long you know 'em."

Mike nodded absently. Some people were a mystery, but until a couple of seconds ago he would have sworn Allie wasn't one of them. She had *a plan*. From the day she'd shown up in his newly opened diner at the age of sixteen, she'd known exactly what she was going to be: a doctor. She maintained this with such intensity that no one had doubted for a minute that she'd reach her goal.

The news had startled him so much he'd forgotten

the job he had to do before it was too late. "Hang on a sec," Mike told Barney. He dialed the wholesaler again, got him on the phone this time and made it quite clear that his meat order must be delivered at once, because Mike's Diner wasn't a vegetarian restaurant. Then we went right back to the topic of Allie.

"Why'd she quit?"

"Dunno. Haven't heard that part yet."

Mike gritted his teeth. That was the frustrating part about small-town gossip. You got just enough of the story to pique your interest before the news dried up. The details would filter in eventually, one at a time, but he wanted to know now. It would take something major to make Allie give up her plan. Flunked out? No way. Stressed out from the work? Nothing had ever stressed out Allie. A disastrous love affair?

"You okay?" Barney shot him a glance—a quick one, because he had food on the grill.

"Yeah," Mike said, and turned his attention back to his own problems.

Maury, one of his brother's foster boys, swung through the back door, ready to start working. "Hey, Mike, Daniel said to tell you Allie Hendricks is back in town."

"I heard," he told the teenager, smiling at him. He was fond of all Daniel's boys, but he and Maury had a special bond—cooking. In fact, Mike didn't know how he'd get along without Maury when school started and he had to reduce his hours.

Maury looked a lot like a St. Bernard and acted a lot like one, too. "Can I start working on the Moroccan chicken?" he asked, practically salivating.

"Chopping the veggies, yes," Mike told him. "Can't cook the chicken until it gets here."

Mike's Diner, *his* diner, had become the most popular eating place in Serenity Valley, an isolated community tucked between two mountain ranges in southern Vermont. His customers came from all three towns that nestled in the valley: LaRocque, where he was located, Holman, the southernmost, and even the biggest, most uppity town, Churchill, which lay across the river. He served all the things people expected to find in a diner, but each evening he offered a chef's special. These specials had become the talk of the valley.

He'd succeeded with the diner. He had a career, he had his family, his older brother, Daniel, and Ian, the younger one. Life was good.

It hadn't always been good. Ignored by his parents, he'd predictably acted out as a teenager. When he got into trouble with the law, they disowned him.

He'd ended up in a juvenile correctional facility where he'd met Daniel and Ian. They couldn't have been more different in appearance and personality, but they'd shared a common goal—to learn from their mistakes and end up as honest, productive citizens.

They'd made it. Daniel was a veterinarian, Ian was a businessman and sheep farmer and Mike had his restaurant. They'd done it by supporting each other, each making sacrifices on the others' behalf, just as brothers would, which had made them decide to become brothers. They'd changed their surnames to Foster, and in the eyes of the world, they *were* brothers. The people of the valley didn't know about their past, and the Fosters wanted to keep it that way. It didn't matter what they'd done as kids. What mattered was what they were doing now.

And at the moment, he wasn't doing a whole lot. He opened at seven, and the pace was frantic until nine.

Then it slowed until just before noon, when everyone worked flat out until two, which gave him plenty of time to get ready for dinner. He had two waitresses, Becky and Colleen, who needed full-time work as much as he needed to know he'd have dependable help.

With Maury on deck, Mike was free to wander around the dining room, giving the customers who were straggling in for an early lunch some personal attention. "Hey, Ray, Ed," he said to two of LaRocque's city selectmen. "Sit anywhere you like. Want a dark corner to conspire in?"

"If you can think of something for us to conspire about," Ray said. "This town could use a good fight."

Mike observed that they weren't speaking to him, but to his forehead. He knew what was coming.

"Like your hair," Ed said. "Glad you stopped shaving it off."

Ray studied Mike's head for a moment as if whether or not Mike grew his hair out was of utmost importance to the community. He finally nodded as well. "Better this way."

"Thank you," Mike said, meaning, *Drop it. Now.* This was another downside of a small town like La-Rocque, Vermont. Anything that could be called news got chewed and worked over and sent phone bills sky-high, and the news right now was that he was letting his hair grow out. He'd just have to live with it until something more exciting came along to put his hair on the back burner, so to speak.

"Did you hear Allie Hendricks is back in town?" Ed asked him.

That was it, the new news. Maybe now that Allie was back in town, people would focus on her rather than his hair.

He took their orders himself, and while he scribbled on the pad, he was thinking about Allie. Smart, friendly, efficient and pretty; well, beautiful in her own way, she'd waitressed for him summers and holidays from the time he'd opened the restaurant eight years ago. He'd seen her through her college years and was both proud and heartbroken—in a selfish way—when she was accepted to medical school. Of course, she was the best waitress he'd ever had. She was also the most overeducated one he'd ever had.

He seated a few more early lunch customers, since Becky and Colleen were setting tables, then went into the kitchen area and perched himself on a stool beside Maury, who was chopping almonds and dried apricots like a pro. The chicken had arrived at last, so Mike began trimming it.

He was working automatically and lost in thought when Becky appeared at his side, beaming. "Allie Hendricks is back in town," she said, "and she's here for lunch."

Surprised at how happy that made him, Mike stood, washed his hands, and went back into the dining room. He looked around for Allie, then took a second look at the stunning brunette who was smiling at him. This was Allie?

Mike suddenly had a burning desire to see if he looked okay with hair, which was dumb. He'd known Allie for years. She was like a little sister. It didn't matter what *he* looked like. It was how *she* looked that threw him.

She looked more mature. More...polished. The bookish, awkward girl he remembered had been replaced by a confident, elegant woman.

He approached her feeling dazed. She'd stopped by

the diner from time to time when she'd been on breaks from college, but when had her transformation happened? The Allie he remembered had sported a bouncy ponytail. Now, sleek dark hair fell to her shoulders, swung forward to frame her face. He couldn't help skimming her up and down—any male would. Her bright-red turtleneck made her skin look translucent and her brown eyes a deeper, more vibrant chocolate-brown. Five-four, five-five, she was slim, but curvy, too. In the black skirt she wore with boots she looked absolutely...female.

When he reached her, he couldn't figure out what to do. A couple of years ago he would have given her a big hug. Now it didn't feel right, so he stuck out his hand and gave her a big-brotherly smile. "Hey, Allie, it's great to see you again."

She raised an eyebrow at his outstretched hand, shook it, then gave him a startled look. "You've let your hair grow."

"Um, yes. And you've let yours down." He felt himself flushing. "I mean..."

She seemed to be trying not to giggle. "Looks great. So how've you been?"

"Good. Fine. Um, good." Mike cleared his throat. He knew he was acting like a dork, but he was confused. Every cell in his body was screaming at him to flirt with this gorgeous woman, but he couldn't. The gorgeous woman was Allie. She was still eight years younger than he was, time didn't change that, but eight years didn't seem like such a big age difference now.

He brought himself back to reality. She was also a woman in the middle of a personal crisis. Something momentous had happened to cause her to drop out of med school. Now was definitely not the time to hit on her.

"So are you home for a while?" He waved her over to one of the booths against the west wall.

She sat and looked up at him. "Yes. And I need a job."

It was the last thing he'd expected her to say. "A job?"

Her smile was rueful. "Yes, that is, if you need help." She glanced around the diner, looking a little less confident all of a sudden. "Actually, it looks as if you already have it under control. I just wanted to check with you first…"

His brain came to life at last. "Of course I'll give you a job," he said as fast as he could get the words out. "Absolutely. No question about it. Only question is, why would you want to be a waitress again?"

With the direct look he'd come to associate with her over the years, she said, "You've probably heard that I've taken a semester off from school to think things through."

It wasn't exactly what he'd heard, but he nodded.

"I need to work, pay my mom rent—"

She must have noticed his surprise, because she said, "No, she hasn't asked me to pay rent. But she's hysterical that I've come home. I just want to—"

"Feel more independent," Mike said.

"Oh, yes." She said the words on a long sigh.

It gave him time to notice how luscious her mouth looked with shiny red lipstick smoothed over it. A wave of awareness washed over him. This wasn't good. He had to keep his hormones in check.

"Thanks, Mike," she said softly. "I hope you're not just doing this because…"

"Because you're the best waitress I've ever had?" He

smiled at her, feeling more in control now. "When can you start?"

"Tonight at the dinner shift?"

He nodded and pushed back from the table, wanting to put some distance between them.

"Thank you again." When she smiled, her skin seemed to glow.

"No problem." He couldn't think of a closing line. Finally he fell back on his standby—food. "How about some pie? I'll send out a piece of chocolate meringue."

"You remembered that was my favorite," she said.

She looked so pleased that he felt uncomfortable again. Aw, hell. It was definitely time to get back to the kitchen. "Of course I remembered."

He signaled Colleen, told her to rush the pie to Allie and then review the new procedures with her. With a final wave in Allie's direction, he retreated to safety. This reaction he was having to Allie was not only surprising, it was annoying.

"Cut it out," he muttered.

"Cut what out?" Maury looked up at him and blinked. "I was just about to start on the carrots."

Mike glanced at Maury's workstation and was amazed to see the progress the boy had already made on the vegetables that would go into tonight's dinner special. He gave the impression that he was taking it slow and easy until you saw what he could accomplish in a short time. He had a real future ahead of him in the culinary arts.

Realizing Maury was still waiting for an answer, Mike said, "Ah, sure, the carrots."

Colleen appeared at the pass-through. "Mike, phone call for you."

Mike stepped into his small office off the kitchen, relieved to have a distraction. "Mike's Diner," he said cheerfully.

"I'm calling for Michael Foster," said a crisp voice with a British accent.

"It's Mike. Speaking," Mike said, pacing back and forth while he was on hold, his mind still on Allie. He glanced into the dining room, saw her laughing with some of the customers, then groaned and ducked back inside the office.

"Mike!" The man on the phone spoke enthusiastically. "Richard Stein here. I'm with Abernathy Foods, and I'm interested in your restaurant."

"It's not for sale," Mike said, and the phone was on its way to the cradle when he heard Stein say, "No, no, I'm quite aware of that."

He put the receiver back to his ear. "You want a reservation?" he asked warily. "We don't take reservations—"

"No," the man said again, adding a lot of ho-ho-ho-ing. "I mean, yes, of course I'd love to have dinner there, but I'm in New York, you see, and don't have a lot of time to…"

"I don't have a lot of time, either, Mr. Stein," Mike said. "I'm in the middle of the lunch crunch."

"This will just take a minute," Stein said. "What I called about was franchising Mike's Diner. I read the great review you got in the *Boston Globe* a few months ago, and we sent a couple of our people to check out your place. They came back with stellar reports. We've run some numbers, and now we'd like you to come to New York, see our operation, talk about the offer—"

"What?" Mike said. He couldn't quite focus on what Stein had just said. Somebody he didn't even know had checked him out and was running numbers on him? What the heck did that mean? And was Allie still out there?

Without thinking, he shifted to the doorway again. Allie was gathering up her bag and her jacket and talking to Colleen and Becky. Almost as if she felt his gaze, she turned to meet it. He raised one hand in goodbye. She smiled and waved back. He wanted to know what "things" Allie was home to "think over" a lot more than he wanted to know what Stein was talking about.

"...interested in franchising your restaurant, opening several others like it. We'd start small, stick to Vermont locations for starters. Then if they're a go, we'd... Mike? We still connected?"

Mike refocused. "Sorry," he said. "Give me your number and I'll call you back. I'm pretty busy right now."

"Sure," Stein said. "Those customers come first, don't they?" He rattled off a number, repeated his name and "Abernathy Foods" a couple of times. Mike jotted down the information on an order pad, even though he probably wouldn't call him back. The idea of franchising didn't appeal to him.

"When can I expect your call?" Stein asked.

Cornered, Mike couldn't bring himself to say, *never.* "Um, two-thirty?"

"Great," Stein said, sounding perfectly happy about being told to wait a couple of hours. "I'll be here."

Still holding the phone, Mike watched Allie hug Becky and Colleen, wave to the friends she'd been chatting with and then leave.

Ay-uh, as the old-time Vermonters said, he was busy all right. Busy thinking about Allie.

"HE GAVE YOU a job." Elaine Hendricks gave her daughter a look that could break even the hardest heart.

At the moment, Allie's heart felt like a big marshmallow in her chest. But she couldn't weaken. "Yes, Mom, Mike hired me. Just now. It's simply amazing that you already know." She took a chance and smiled.

Elaine merely sniffed and kept on with that look. "It was very kind of him, too," Allie continued, "because I don't think he really needed anyone."

"No, he didn't."

"How do you know *that?*" This time Allie tried for a teasing tone.

Another sniff. Worse, Allie observed, her mother was baking, which she'd always said was cheaper than a psychiatrist. Steadily, she forged ahead. "I'm grateful, too, because I'll be able to handle my personal expenses and pay you a smidgen of rent."

A pan of her legendary sugar cookies in her hand, Elaine said, "I don't want rent! I don't want you to be a waitress. Aren't you a little *overeducated* for that?"

The reference to her education filled Allie with guilt. When her father died, he'd left her mother enough to live modestly. Allie knew her college years had required sacrifices over and above the scholarships she'd been given. Still, she couldn't get caught up in a guilt trip. She'd feel even guiltier if she went back to med school and ended up being an incompetent doctor. She said calmly, "I need things to do and a little money coming in while I decide what career I really want to pursue."

"A medical career! It's what you've always wanted."

"It *was* what I'd always wanted," Allie said quietly. "Turns out I was wrong."

"What you'll do is settle back into the valley, never

want to leave, be a waitress for the rest of your life," her mother said sadly. "I've seen it happen to plenty of people."

"Even if I turn into one of them, may I still have a cookie?" Allie asked, and in return, got a look that sent her scampering up to her room with a stack of cookies and a mug of tea sloshing perilously as she ran.

When she was a kid, her bedroom had been her oasis, although then she'd never felt alone and thirsty in the desert the way she did now. As a child, she'd adored her parents, and after her father died, she'd become even closer to her mother. Until now, when a stone wall had risen between them.

Not even her room felt the same. Being home was strange, like trying to wear clothes she'd outgrown. The tension between her mother and her made it so much worse.

She'd come home without calling to avoid the inevitable argument as long as possible, but now she felt she hadn't done the right thing. Her mother had been shocked, shocked by Allie's sudden appearance, shocked by her decision to take a semester off to reflect on her medical career, and a shocked mother, apparently, was a mother playing motherhood for all it was worth.

"How could you do this?" she'd sobbed piteously. "How could you throw away a promising career?"

"I didn't throw it away. I just need some time to think."

Logic and explanation hadn't calmed her mother in the least. Resigned, Allie searched her closet, hoping to find the black slacks and white shirts she'd worn to waitress at Mike's restaurant for so many years.

There they were, clean, starched and perfectly ironed. That was the kind of mother she had—or was until

Allie had disappointed her by wanting to rethink being a doctor.

After she found the clothes, she took a good hard look at her room. It was exactly as it was when she'd left it for college—pink and flowery. The cloying peony-printed wallpaper was half-hidden with pictures of friends, dried corsages, party invitations dating back to first grade, camp awards, school awards, her Phi Beta Kappa key, diplomas—her entire past, such as it was. As for the present, nothing in the room indicated the person she was now.

Not that she had a clue as to who that woman was. All her life, Allie had known what she wanted to do. She'd chosen a path and stuck to it industriously until a few months ago, when, engaged in a special summer project, she'd finally confronted the truth—it was the wrong path. It would lead to a job she'd never be able to do well enough to satisfy her need to do everything perfectly.

It had turned her world upside-down. She'd spent the summer thinking about it, examining her feelings, talking to a counselor, before she made her decision. While she'd told her mother that she just needed a while to think things over, she'd already decided not to go back to med school.

She pushed aside the panic that overtook her each time she realized what she'd done. She'd figure it out, find a new path and start walking it with the same industrious spirit she'd always had.

It wasn't the end of the road for her. Just a detour.

She was buttoning her white shirt when she heard the tap on her door. "Come in, Mom," she called out, thinking, *What now? How much more guilt can she heap on me?*

Elaine sat down on the edge of the bed. She was such a pretty woman, Allie thought, as blond as Allie was brunette, a bit plump from all those years of cooking and baking. She had a smooth, even temperament—until yesterday, when Allie had popped in with her bad news. Elaine Hendricks would never surprise or shock anyone. She...

"I've been thinking," her mother said slowly, "and I want to tell you a story."

Allie's fingers stopped with a shirt button half-pushed in. *About a girl who didn't do what her mother said and turned into an iguana?*

"Before I married your father," Elaine said, "I got cold feet."

Okay, this was a surprise. "You did not," Allie protested. "You told me the first time you laid eyes on Dad you knew he was *the one*."

"Yes, until that engagement ring was on my finger. Then I started wondering if I was doing the right thing." She pursed her lips as if she were reliving that moment of doubt. "My mother was fitting my wedding dress on me—I'll never forget it—and when she started fastening it up the back, I said, 'Stop.' I stepped out of the dress, packed a bag, cashed in the bonds my grandmother had left me and went to Las Vegas."

Allie's head swam. "Las Vegas?"

"I tanned by the pool, read romances, watched sitcoms about perfect families and just worked at feeling young. But I also talked to newlywed women, and to the ones who were there to get divorces, listening to their stories of deciding they'd found the right man, and the stories from the divorcées about how they'd been wrong."

Allie nodded. No need to feel tense. She knew how the story ended.

"What was Dad doing while you were…thinking?"

"He called me every night, asking me if I was ready to come home, and each time, I told him I wasn't sure yet. Then one day I was at the pool reading, felt someone watching me, looked up and there he was. 'I need to do some thinking, too,' he said. He plopped himself down on the lounge chair beside mine, and the rest is history."

The import of the story hit Allie at last. She sat on the bed beside her mother, put an arm around her shoulders and said, "You ran away. Just like me."

Elaine nodded ruefully. "That's what occurred to me this morning. I ran away, so why was I so shocked when you did the same thing?"

"Well, you were—"

"I was being hypocritical. I'm sorry."

"But after you ran, you ended up making the right decision, don't you think?" Allie said, remembering her tall, handsome, kind father whose dark eyes showed only love for her and her mother.

"Oh, yes," Elaine said. "And you will, too, sweetheart."

"Thanks, Mom," Allie said, hugging her tight.

"When I was remembering how lazy I was in Vegas," Elaine said, and smiled at last, "I thought about you and how *you'd* started by getting a job. So I wondered if you might like to take on some volunteer work, too."

"Sure," Allie said, so relieved she'd have been willing to shovel manure for an elderly dairy farmer. "What is it?"

"Lilah Foster, Daniel's new wife and a lovely woman,

is planning a benefit dinner to raise funds for the Serenity Valley Foster Care Center."

"The place Daniel's building?"

"Yes. A community of separate houses, each with a 'mother' and 'father' to provide the closest thing to a real home for foster children."

"That's a worthy cause," Allie murmured.

"I'm chairing the finance committee, getting donations from local businesses. She needs somebody to arrange the actual dinner—food, rentals, decorations, all that—for the benefit. Mike's catering, so you're the logical person to volunteer."

At the mention of Mike's name, Allie's mind wandered. He'd looked good today, very handsome, very confident. She'd been happy to see him again, and she was looking forward to working with him at the diner. Being around him would be good for her. He was such a focused person himself that he might be able to help her figure out what she wanted to do with her life.

She smiled back at her mother. "Better than getting a tan—better for your skin *and* your conscience. It sounds like fun, Mom. Happy to do it."

"Good. Lilah will be pleased." Elaine went to the door, then said, "You know, they always say to ask the busiest person you know to take on a volunteer job, and our new ophthalmologist is working with me on the fundraising committee. I'll make sure you get to chat with her."

Nope, Allie thought as she fastened her last two buttons, her mother hadn't given up yet on the hope that Allie's "right decision" would be to become a doctor after all.

Chapter Two

Several minutes after Stein's call, life at the diner was back to normal. Becky and Colleen gave staccato orders over the pass-through to the kitchen, Barney filled them with astounding speed, and Mike cooked. The phone rang several times, but Mike shut the sound out of his head and gave the food his full attention—except for those moments his mind wandered toward Allie.

He wished he'd asked her to start tomorrow night, or on the weekend, to give him time to get over the impact of seeing her looking so different. On the other hand, maybe when he saw her in her old uniform of black pants and white shirt, she'd look like the Allie he knew. The Allie he thought of as a kid.

He'd really be grateful if she'd put her hair up in a ponytail.

At one-thirty, Becky ran into the kitchen. "Mike, there's a lawyer on the phone for you. Says it's urgent."

Had Stein mentioned he was a lawyer for Abernathy Foods? He hadn't said what he was. Had to be the same person. "I told him I'd call him back at two-thirty," Mike said, distracted by his pans of sautéing vegetables. "Tell him again. Two-thirty's the best I can do."

"But he—"

"It's okay, Becky." He smiled at her. "Tell him I *told* you to tell him."

Looking worried, Becky went back to the desk.

As soon as Maury went to the storeroom to inventory staples, Barney yelled over the sizzle of hamburgers, "What's going on?"

Mike turned off the burners under the vegetables. He sure couldn't yell back, not news like this. "Some guy from New York called and wants to franchise the diner."

"Franchise the diner?" Barney said, making it sound like *burn down the diner?*

"Yeah. What do you think?"

Barney scratched his chef's hat, the closest he could get to his head when he was cooking. "Well, I don't know."

"Thanks," Mike said. "That helps."

"I mean, I don't know enough about it yet, and my guess is you don't, either. So when you do, ask me again, and do some explaining first."

"That's actually good advice," Mike admitted. "This guy wants me to come to New York to hear about the offer."

"I guess you'd better go."

"Think you and Maury can hold down the fort?"

Barney raised his eyebrows. "I never did need you," he said, "and that kid's just waiting for a chance to get you out of his kitchen."

Mike laughed. "Yeah, I know. And if the food's even halfway okay—"

"The customers'll be calling him out for a round of applause. So don't get jealous."

AT LAST, the lunch crowd cleared out except for a few stragglers in need of nothing more than a cup of coffee and a piece of pie. Becky and Colleen came in to say they were leaving for a while, and Becky said, "Promise me you'll call the lawyer. I left his number on the message pad. He sounded as if he really needed to talk to you."

"I have the number." He wandered back into the kitchen, not feeling his usual excitement about finishing things up for dinner. He'd said he'd call Stein at two-thirty, and for some reason he was dreading it.

He felt unprepared for a conversation about franchising. What did he know about it? A couple of McDonald's, a couple of Starbucks, then they multiplied like rabbits. The hamburgers and the coffee tasted the same in each one. That was the extent of his knowledge.

But it wouldn't be the extent of Ian's knowledge. Ian was the businessman of their self-made family. He'd know if anybody did. Mike glanced at the clock above the huge commercial range. Two-twenty. He had time. Ian didn't talk much. Quickly he punched in the number.

He was in luck. Ian was at home. "Abernathy Foods wants to franchise the diner," he said without even saying hello.

"Wow," Ian said. His flat tone was as excited as Ian ever sounded. "You've hit the big time."

"I guess," Mike said, "but I don't know anything about franchising. Can you fill me in?"

"A company likes the looks of an operation, they buy the name and concept and then start selling franchises. You'll get rich and they'll get richer."

"Rich would be good," Mike admitted.

"You'd have to pay a price, though. You'll be the founder of the chain, but the *company* will select the franchisees. The *company* will lay down the rules, and you'll have to follow them just like the other franchisees. If Abernathy Foods is publicly owned, a board of directors, the management and a whole bunch of shareholders will have the right to tell you to put sugar in your tomato sauce."

"The board of directors talks about recipes?"

Ian blew out a breath. "No. It was just an example."

"Oh." Mike stopped frantically taking notes and thought about somebody else making decisions about his restaurant. "It might be nice for a while," he said. "I could make us all rich, sit back on my tush, get some rest, travel…"

"Or they might hire you to organize the franchise, lay down those rules—with the approval, of course, of the marketing department, the CFO, the CEO—"

"And the board," Mike said, feeling dizzy. "Doesn't sound like my thing, does it?"

"No. But we're way ahead of ourselves. Call them back and ask questions. While you're talking, I'll do some research, find out if Abernathy Foods is worth talking to."

"You're sure you have time to do this?" Ian handled the family's business affairs and managed a flock of merino sheep. He stayed busy.

"I have time. For some people."

Mike heard an almost-smile in his voice. Ian had time for him. When the three of them had cast their lots with each other, he'd found out what family was.

He put down the phone, and immediately it rang. If Maury hadn't been around—he seemed to have given up on getting any help from Mike and was forging ahead with the cooking himself—Mike would have uttered a vile curse. "Mike's Diner," he said less cheerfully than usual.

"Where the heck is Maury?"

It was the Churchill Consolidated High School football coach, sounding belligerent. "He's right here, coach," Mike said. "Want to talk to him?"

"No, I don't wanna talk to him. I want you to tell me why he's there instead of over here, in Churchill, at *football practice*."

Maury hadn't mentioned football practice, but Mike didn't intend to tattle. "Is it time?" he asked innocently. "I guess we were so busy we lost track. Don't worry. I'll be sure he gets there tomorrow."

"Not tomorrow, today," the coach thundered. "He's my star linebacker. Or he will be, *if* he comes to practice! Tell him to get over here right now."

The man had his priorities straight, for sure. "I think I can manage without him now that the worst is over," Mike conceded. "He'll be there."

Maury had started browning chicken and was staring really hard at it. Mike pulled a stool up to the huge range.

"Maury, Maury," he began, shaking his head. "What am I going to do with you?"

"I've been busted," Maury said. "I'm sorry, but you told me about the Moroccan chicken, and I just had to see how to…"

Mike held up a silencing hand. "I know. It's in your blood. You'll be a five-star chef someday, but, Maury, first you have get through high school."

Maury was sharp as a well-honed knife, but it had "taken a village," which meant their entire extended family all the way down to Daniel's youngest foster boys, to help maintain Maury's C-average. He'd been working at the restaurant weekends and holidays from the time Daniel took him in, and now that he had his driver's license, he was here every second he didn't have to be somewhere else. And today, apparently, when he *was* supposed to be somewhere else.

"Look at it this way," Mike explained. "You're conscientious about being here because you know I have to get dinner on the table. You have to be just as conscientious about football practice, because the coach has to get a team on the field. Preferably a good team."

"Yeah," Maury said. "I get it." Reluctantly he removed the last of the browned chicken from the pan, moved the pan off the burner, carefully wiped his knife, and less carefully, wiped his hands. "Guess I'd better go." He gave Mike a smile and a wave. "Later."

With that crisis settled, Mike had no excuse for postponing the call to Stein. At the front desk he found two numbers placed on the cash register where he couldn't possibly miss them, the one he'd written on the order form and another in Becky's handwriting on a proper message pad. He dialed the one he'd written down and was surprised when Stein himself answered. That explained the two numbers. This was Stein's private line.

"Mike!" he said as if Santa Claus had just landed on the chimney hearth.

"Sorry I couldn't take your other call," Mike said. "We'd agreed on two-thirty."

Stein was silent for a moment. "I didn't make another call." And then, "Somebody else called you about franchising?"

He sounded so anxious that Mike wanted to reassure him. "No. I don't know what he was calling about. Are you a lawyer with Abernathy Foods?"

"No. I'm vice-president of acquisitions."

"He was a lawyer. So he was calling about something entirely different."

But what? He glanced at the other number and saw the Boston area code and the name Earl Ritter at the top. Lawyers made him nervous. So did the police. He'd had reason to be nervous when he was a kid, committing one petty crime after another. But not now. Not unless something from his past had come back to haunt him.

Everything else seemed inconsequential now. The call from that lawyer—urgent, Becky had said—could be the big one.

He made himself calm down. The man he was talking to now wanted to make him rich, or to make himself rich, at least. To stick to diners instead of doom, Mike consulted the notes he'd written on Ian's instructions. "Tell me more about your proposal," he said through the cottony dryness of his mouth.

He listened to Stein drone on about "buying the concept, positioning the product"—which Mike took to be the diner—telling him pretty much what Ian had. He finished up with, "Those are the bare bones of the plan. Come to New York, we'll show you around corporate headquarters, give you a more visual idea of what we have in mind. Any questions?"

"Yes. What other franchises do you control?"

After a second of silence, maybe startled silence because he hadn't expected any sort of intelligent response from the owner of Mike's Diner in LaRocque, Vermont, Stein rattled off an impressive list of big names in fast-food. Not that Mike would eat at any of them if he didn't have to, but he knew they were successful.

"How much input will I have into the plan for the diner franchises?"

"As much as you like!" Stein said heartily. "We're

going to pay you a lot of money. Don't think we're going to let you off the hook." A riff of ho-ho-ho followed.

"Will I have any say in quality control?"

"Well, not directly, unless you'd like to work for us in that capacity. That's a great idea, come to think of it," Stein said with enthusiasm. "We'll talk about it."

Since that idea didn't appeal to him at all, Mike swiftly went on to his next question. "The concept, as you put it, is an ordinary diner with an extraordinary dinner special," Mike said. "It's different every night. Can you do the same thing with a string of franchises?"

"To some extent," Stein said. Mike could tell he was hedging. "Might not be able to do a different one every night of the world, but... Hey, my friend," he said, hearty again, "these are details we can go into in depth later on. Now, about coming to New York for a visit with us..."

Mike thought for a few seconds, a long few seconds. He'd figured out how he could leave the diner for a day or two, cook ahead, write out detailed instructions, then pray quietly to the gods of good food that nothing went wrong. "I could do that. I couldn't stay long."

"We'll have our presentation so well-organized it won't take long," Stein said. "When can you come? Next week? Wednesday sound good?"

"I have to check some dates," Mike said. "I'll call you back tomorrow."

"I'll call you," Stein sang. "What about five or so this afternoon?"

Mike was getting the not-unpleasant feeling that Stein *really* wanted to franchise his diner. Maybe it would be a good thing. He wouldn't have to feel under so much pressure all the time. He'd increase the financial status of his family. But... "I'll try to have an answer for you by then," he said.

As soon as the call with Stein ended, he called Ian. "Unless you tell me not to," he said, "I'm going to New York to talk to these people."

"Good," Ian said. "Successful company, give it a shot."

"I will." Then he added, "I also have to return a phone call from a lawyer in Boston."

"So?"

"*So?* So maybe it's bad news."

Ian made a huffing noise. "Why would you assume that?"

"You know why." Mike knew Ian thought he was being an idiot, and maybe he was. He looked at the phone number again. "I should stop second-guessing and just make the call."

"Well, yeah."

After saying goodbye to Ian, Mike picked up the message pad and dialed. He and his brothers had been living honest, productive lives since they'd left juvenile correction. Seriously, what was the worst the folks around here could do if they found out they weren't brothers by birth? Find a vet outside the valley? Stop eating at the diner? Stop wearing wool?

That was enough to make him smile.

"Mike Foster," he said crisply when an assistant answered, "returning Mr. Ritter's call."

"Oh, yes, Mr. Foster." Rather than being coolly professional, she sounded distraught. "Mr. Ritter's been called away on a family emergency. He was very anxious to speak with you, but I've just discovered he left his BlackBerry behind, so I can't give you a cell number."

"No problem," Mike said, his stomach muscles clenching. "I'll wait to hear from him." No smiling now. He'd wanted so badly to get it over with, whatever it was, and now he'd have to worry about it for hours, days, maybe.

He put the phone down slowly. He had to call Stein back about going to New York. He'd have to get through the dinner rush, smiling, chatting, and twisted like a licorice stick inside. It wouldn't help that Allie would be there waiting tables, either, but maybe the annoying attraction he'd felt this morning wouldn't come back. Instead, it would feel like old times having her around.

And she might take his mind off both the lawyer and the franchise deal. Tonight he just wanted to run his restaurant.

ALLIE COULDN'T BELIEVE how quickly it all came back to her. Working at the diner felt as comfortable as the old black flats she'd worn to work. She'd quickly picked up the changes to the menu, and the new cash register was a snap to figure out.

The only downside was that she knew almost everyone who came into the restaurant. And *everyone* wanted to know the same thing—what was she doing working at Mike's Diner? Why wasn't she in medical school?

Except that Vermonters didn't ask people about their private lives. Not directly. Instead, they said, "Allie, heard you were home," their eyebrows lifted almost to the hairline, hoping she'd explain. When she said cheerfully, "It's great to be back. Let me tell you about the dinner special," the next prod was something like, "How's med school?" And when all she said was, "The university has a great medical school. The special tonight is…" her cross-examiner would say, "Bet your mom's glad to have you home."

At which she would smile and blurt out the special, then speed away.

Several times during the evening she'd managed to say hi to Mike, or send him a little wave, but hadn't had a chance to have a conversation with him. The diner was swamped. At eight, business started to slow down. Allie carried a stack of plates into the kitchen and observed that Mike was in his office.

"Busy night," she said, just tossing it into the room, not wanting to disturb his work at the computer.

Instead of ignoring her, Mike swiveled his desk chair toward her. "How're you doing, kiddo?"

She knew he was talking about more than her first night back at the diner. "Okay." When he kept looking at her, she admitted, "You know, half relieved that I made a move to save myself, half scared to death that I'll regret it. But I'll be fine. I have things to keep me busy. One of them is that I've agreed to chair the dinner committee for the benefit."

"Your mother sucked you in?"

"Afraid so." It was true, but she hated to admit it. "I'm so glad you're catering it."

"What choice did I have?" he said. "In fact, what choice did my sister-inlaw have when she was planning the benefit? But the good news here," he added, "is that it sounds like you and Elaine are speaking to each other, at least."

"Yes, thank goodness. She more or less apologized for overreacting, but I know what she's hoping I'll decide."

"Your mom's a stubborn woman."

Allie jumped. She hadn't noticed Barney standing behind her.

"She'll come around," Barney said, and then added, "Just wanted you to know we served all the whatever it was, the chicken special." He turned and went back to his after-dinner, pre-breakfast jobs.

"Barney knows my mother?" Allie asked Mike. "I mean, well enough to know she's stubborn?"

"News to me," Mike said. "By the way," he asked her, "what's the date of the benefit? Nobody tells me anything."

She named a date in late October. "Any problem?"

"Nope." He gave her an odd look, then blurted out, "Want to come to breakfast tomorrow morning and talk about the menu?"

"Sure," Allie said, surprised by the suggestion, but strangely excited, too. "Breakfast would be great." With a wave, she went back to cleaning up the dining room with Colleen and Becky.

A few words with Mike, and she already felt better. What was it about him? For one thing, he was consistently calm and unruffled. In spite of his bright green eyes and his short, almost military-style auburn hair that indicated some fighting Irish in his blood, she'd never seen him lose his temper.

Hold it back, maybe, but never lose it.

Maybe it was because he was happy with his life. He'd found his calling. Mike and food. They went together like love and red roses.

And what went together with her? She'd learned she wasn't meant to be a dedicated doctor. She'd always thought it was what she wanted to do with her life until she actually began to study medicine. First she'd had that calm, "I'll start to enjoy it later," feeling. Next came doubt, then disinterest. She'd had to force herself to retain her rigorous study habits, her intense focus on being at the top of the class. But at last, she'd been overwhelmed by boredom.

That was when she knew she could never be the kind of doctor a patient deserved.

Sooner or later, she'd figure out what she did want to do. In the meantime, she'd work at the diner and throw the best party—the benefit dinner—Serenity Valley had ever seen.

For now, it was enough.

AFTER ALLIE walked away, Mike groaned. *Breakfast.* He'd asked her to meet him for breakfast. Had he lost his mind? The entire time she'd been talking to him, he'd been thinking big-bad-wolf thoughts that surprised him even more than they might surprise her. In his current state of uncertainty about how to treat an adult, attractive, no, *desirable* Allie, he should have suggested they discuss the benefit menu by phone, e-mail and fax.

Anything but in person.

Maybe the upcoming trip to New York would help. He'd be gone for a couple of days, and the change might do him good. Deliberately pushing thoughts of Allie out of his mind, he considered which dinner specials Barney and Maury could handle while he was in New York. Then he went back to worrying about the lawyer.

Twenty-four hours ago everything was fine. Allie was happy in med school, or so he'd thought, instead of running around the diner in a starched white shirt and black trousers that weren't too tight, but they weren't loose, either. Nobody was bugging him to franchise the diner and coming to New York to discuss it. Maury wasn't cutting football practice to learn how to make Moroccan chicken. Lawyers weren't calling and then not being around to explain why they'd called.

He wished it would all just go away.

At a little after ten, he locked up and wearily climbed

the stairs to his apartment over the diner. It was such a relief not to be pretending anymore that life was just hunky-dory. He poured a glass of wine, hoping it would make him sleepy, and collapsed on the sofa.

His eyelids drooped. He stifled a yawn. Just as he was dropping off to sleep, he heard the phone in the diner ring. He didn't even try to make it downstairs to catch it before the fourth ring. He needed his rest.

He needed to be alert—and cautious—when he saw Allie in the morning.

Chapter Three

When Allie breezed into the diner, she brought with her the hint of autumn in the air, the scent of wood smoke and apples. She was wearing black slacks that skimmed her slender hips and a sparkling white shirt.

"You're wearing your uniform?" Mike asked her.

"In case you needed extra help," she said as she came up to him, all smiles, her eyes glowing. "I wanted to be dressed appropriately."

"Thanks, but we can't have you working around the clock." Mike couldn't help smiling back. Even though he knew it was selfish, knew that Allie should be a hundred and fifty miles away in school, he was glad she was here temporarily and working for him. "What if I started to depend on you? Because when you decide what you want to do with your life, I insist that you desert me."

"Don't worry." Her eyes narrowed. "The second I decide what to do next, I'll be out of here so fast you won't even have a chance to say goodbye."

"Sure you will." When Allie left—and she would—she wouldn't just desert him, and they both knew it. He led her to a table in the back. "Want a menu?"

Her eyes twinkled. "I have one, thank you, branded on my memory. The special last night was wonderful, by the way."

"Thanks," he said. "It nearly cost Maury his position on the football team."

Before he could explain away her puzzled expression, Colleen and Becky, both stout and motherly, descended on their table.

"Coffee?" Becky asked, pouring without waiting for an answer.

"Mike?" Colleen looked surprised. "You're eating?"

"I do, occasionally," he said, "standing up in the kitchen. It's me sitting down that scares you."

She giggled, opened her order pad and turned to Allie. "Gosh, we're glad to have you back with us," she said. "It's just like old times."

"Good to be home for a while," Allie said.

"What's for breakfast, you skinny little thing?" Colleen asked fondly.

"Everything," Allie said. "Eggs over easy, bacon, home fries, whole wheat toast—"

"We're serving biscuits now," Colleen said. "A Southern touch. Want to try one? Barney thinks he's finally got the recipe just right."

"Absolutely. Maybe I *should* look at a menu if you're changing things around here."

Mike ordered the same thing, added juice for both of them and instructed Colleen to bring out cinnamon rolls as soon as the next batch was out of the oven.

"That's more than I eat in a week," Allie protested.

"Good thing you're home so we can feed you. How *are* things at home?"

"Everything's fine except that I feel even guiltier now that Mom's not hysterical anymore," Allie said. "I've disappointed her, and she makes gingerbread for me. I've dashed her hopes and dreams for me, and this morning she brought me coffee in bed." She sighed. "I'm being killed by kindness."

Mike laughed. "Maybe she feels guilty for being so upset when you came home."

"Could be. It seems she ran away once."

She told him about Elaine fleeing to Vegas. He was astounded. He could have sworn Elaine Hendricks had never done anything reckless her entire life. "That's an eye-opener," he said when Allie'd finished. "So she has to understand, right?"

"Ah, but the point is," Allie said, "that she came to her senses and married my father. The parallel—" and she gestured dramatically as a lecturer might "—is for me to come to my senses and go back to med school."

Mike couldn't imagine how it would feel to have a parent in his court the way Elaine was in Allie's court, but he did know how terrible he'd feel if he let down someone he cared about. "It's none of my business, but what made you decide to quit?"

"A lot of things," she told him. "Not enjoying the work, being bored by it. I tried hard, but my grades weren't up to my standards. Not bad, just..."

"A three-point-five average instead of a four?"

She cleared her throat. "Three-point-seven," and when she saw how much that amused him, she said defensively, "but when you've made all As for twelve years and a four-point grade average in college, it's not enough."

Mike nodded. She'd always been a perfectionist, even when she was folding paper napkins in the diner. "Just remember it's your decision," he told her. "Sooner or later you'll find your four-point field."

When he realized he was holding her gaze too long to call it "making eye contact," he forced himself to look away. What was he doing here? This was not good. Allie was a friend. He was eight years older than she was. He'd known her since she was a kid.

He had to cut it out.

"...better be sooner" she was saying when his mind stopped wandering and he started listening again. "I have to make a fresh start at the beginning of the second semester. I just *have* to."

Mike nodded, fiddling with his napkin to keep his eyes off her face. "You will. You did the right thing," he said, and there he was, gazing at her again. "You figured out you'd made a mistake and you did something about it before you invested too much in it to quit."

"I guess," she said, "but I feel better when I have a plan."

"You'll have a new plan in no time at all." He had to stop wanting to touch her. He was behaving like an idiot. So he'd start babbling like an idiot instead. "I'd always wanted to be a chef, and when I got tired of being yelled at by pretentious chefs dreaming up pretentious food to serve to pretentious people, I decided instead to open a down-home diner. I was scared out of my wits. What if I replumbed this place, redid the electrical system, decorated it and bought all that kitchen equipment— and then it failed? My only option would have been to drown myself in vinaigrette."

Instead of laughing, she looked at him in a way that made his heart pound. "But you didn't fail. The diner's doing great."

Something in her voice touched him. She sounded as proud as if the diner belonged to her. "Yeah, actually it is. I don't know why or how."

"I do." She smiled. "Great food, a staff that loves working for you..."

"I work them to the bone," he said.

"So I've noticed." Her smile was warm and rich.

Scrounging desperately for some impersonal small talk and coming up with nothing, he was deeply relieved when their breakfast plates showed up. It pleased him no end to see how enthusiastically Allie dug in.

"THIS BISCUIT is too good to be true," Allie said, spreading the homemade strawberry preserves Mike bought from a local woman on top of enough butter to block even the healthiest aorta. "Barney got it right for sure."

"Want another one?"

"No, please, no. I'm going to have to run to Holman and back to work off this one."

She was glad to be home. Glad to be working for Mike. Hanging around with him had always made her feel good about herself. He teased her, laughed with her—he was like the big brother she'd never had.

Yes, just like a brother. She'd been, thank goodness, a sensible enough girl not to get a crush on her boss, so they'd had an easy friendship. She hoped they could go right back to it as if time hadn't passed, but she realized she was noticing things about him now that she hadn't all those years ago. How green his eyes were. That his light-brown lashes were thick and long. That his body was lean but powerful-looking, and his shoulders had that broad, muscular look that made you feel safe when he was around.

She suddenly didn't feel safe and dragged her thoughts away from Mike's body. He'd invited her to breakfast to talk about menus, and she felt it was definitely time to get started. "I'm so glad you can cater the benefit dinner. It'll be an affair to remember."

Good grief, could she have said anything more Freudian? She'd never for a moment dreamed of having an affair with Mike. She barreled on. "I haven't spoken to Daniel's wife about the details yet, but it'll be a seated dinner, so the sky's the limit where the menu is concerned. I thought we'd spend about forty-five minutes just standing around talking, so do you think some simple hors d'oeuvres would be in order? We'll hire valley kids to serve, of course—"

Mike was listening intently, the gleam of his amazing eyes heightened by the morning sun coming through the windows. "Yes, definitely hors d'oeuvres, scattered around on a few tables. Incidentally, the food and labor will be my contribution, so don't worry about the cost. I was thinking beef Wellington, potatoes Anna, roasted asparagus, sautéed grape tomatoes as a surprise, an endive salad to start and a knock-'em-dead dessert that I haven't figured out yet. Oh, yes, and our homemade bread. It's a gourmet take on meat and potatoes. What do you think?"

Her eyes met his. "It sounds perfect."

He smiled. For a long moment, he gazed at her, catching and holding her attention. She couldn't look away. Then some spark, some indefinable awareness passed between them.

At last, Mike cleared his throat and looked away, shattering the sensation. He turned the conversation back to the benefit dinner menu, but Allie wasn't really listening. Something odd had just happened, something personal, unsettling. A pull of attraction had danced between them. She'd never felt anything remotely like that before with Mike, and she didn't like it. Now wasn't the time to do anything reckless. She liked him. He was a friend. That was all.

She realized with a start that Mike had stopped talking. He was looking at her with a puzzled expression on his face.

"That's good," she said quickly.

"Good that I'm worried about Barney's health?"

Allie blinked. Yikes. She hadn't heard a word he'd said about Barney. "No. I mean, yes. Yes, I think it's good of you to worry about him if he's working too hard. Maybe you should talk to him, see if you can get him to take some time off."

He looked even more curious. "You okay?"

Other than the fact that she had no idea what career she was going to pursue and now she was finding herself attracted to one of her oldest friends, everything was just terrific.

"I'm fine. Just distracted. Too much has happened in the last couple of days." She stopped talking, no longer certain what to say next.

He came to her rescue. "That's understandable."

He smiled at her again, and this time, her heart actually seemed to flutter. Good grief! What in the world was wrong with her?

"Cinnamon rolls, right out of the oven," Colleen said, appearing beside the table.

Allie had never been so happy to see another person. "Thank God," she said, realizing too late she'd said it aloud.

Mike and Colleen stared at her as if they thought she'd lost her mind. She couldn't blame them. It definitely was a possibility.

"Guess you really need these," Colleen teased her. "I didn't realize it was a cinnamon-roll emergency."

Allie shot a glance at each of them, feeling her face

heat up, then reached out and grabbed a roll, hoping it would restore her sanity.

There was no doubt about it. She needed to go back to school. Fast.

WHEN ALLIE LEFT, Mike felt the room had dimmed, as if somebody had closed the curtains. Had she wanted to stay longer? He couldn't tell. At some point in the conversation she'd gone off into her own world, had gotten jumpy and nervous.

Which had made him feel jumpy and nervous. He missed the old days, when he could relax around her. This new Allie, grown-up and gorgeous, made him uncomfortable.

He hated it.

The FedEx delivery person came through the door as Mike was on his way back to his office. The packet had come from Abernathy Foods, Inc.

He signed for the envelope and opened it. Plane tickets from Burlington to New York. Notification from a car service he'd had no idea was available in Vermont that a driver would pick him up at eight Wednesday morning to take him to the airport, and yet another statement regarding the driver who would pick him up at JFK airport in New York to take him to the St. Regis Hotel.

Clearly, Abernathy Foods was sparing no expense.

Also included was an itinerary: who he'd meet with, and when, and why.

Should he even consider franchising? Could he really let other people get involved in his diner?

He had no idea what to do. All he knew was that he had too many things to worry about at the same time and it was addling his mind.

ALLIE'S INSIDES were churning with uncertainty and tension as she left the diner. The meeting hadn't gone well. She only hoped she wouldn't act the same way when she came to work later that afternoon.

She had enough going on without getting sappy about Mike. She was grateful to him for giving her a job. Gratitude. That's what it was.

Okay, he was a good-looking guy, but she knew lots of good-looking guys.

Maybe she was just tired. Life with her mother and father, then just her mother, had been a protective cocoon, but now she was a butterfly, out in the real world where she had to make her own way.

She couldn't go on living at home. Her maturity would regress five years in a week. Her mother would treat her as she had when Allie was a child, cooking for her, doing her laundry, cleaning her room. It was already happening, in fact. She'd stepped out of the shower this morning to find her bed already made, and the few clothes she'd put in the hamper were gone.

Could she even afford a place of her own? It wouldn't hurt to look, would it? She bought a copy of the local newspaper, sat down on one of the old-fashioned benches that were placed here and there on Main Street and turned directly to the classified ads for apartments.

"Top flr twnhse, furn…"

She was familiar with the row of townhouses at the bottom of Hubbard Hill. They were new and cheaply built. She'd hate to think how they were furnished.

"Room for rent at…"

No thanks. If she didn't need independence and solitude, she'd stay at home with her mother. There were so few rental offerings that they took about a minute to skim. She knew every house, every apartment in town, and knew none of those few in the paper would meet her needs, even if she could afford them. The decent places were snapped up as soon as they came on the market.

She sighed, got up from the bench and began walking, not aiming for any destination in particular. She reached the library and paused. Libraries always soothed her soul, made her forget the world outside.

She wandered in, tempted to go to the children's section and relive the books she'd loved way back when, but something drew her to the computer. She typed in "health care professions" and watched a list of books appear on the screen. None of the books that interested her was on the shelves, which didn't surprise her. She'd have to request some.

She noticed the head librarian walking her way, so she ducked into the stacks. She didn't want to hear yet again how *surprised* everyone in town was to see Allie Hendricks back at home. And how *stunned* they were that she'd left medical school, and how *amazed* they felt that she'd done something so terrible to her wonderful mother.

Hey, nobody in town was more surprised, stunned or amazed than she was.

She wandered the aisles for a few minutes, looking for the what-to-do-with-your-life section. She could use a book or two on that topic. Not finding any, it occurred to her to check the Psychology section. She could surely use a little counseling. As she skimmed the titles, one book seemed to jump out at her. The title was, *Get a Grip: Understanding Your Emotions*.

She flipped through it, seeing discussions on transference, projecting and other psychological terms with which she wasn't familiar.

Suddenly she realized what was going on with Mike.

In a psychology class she took in undergraduate school, they'd talked about how people often confuse their emotions. For instance, sometimes a person would transfer what they were feeling about one person to another person. Or what they were feeling in one situation to another situation. Often they'd fall in love with their therapists simply because the therapists had helped them with their problems.

Exactly what she was doing with Mike. He was helping her deal with her problems. She was confusing her gratitude with something else. It was as simple as that.

What a relief. Now that she understood what was going on, she'd be able to see him as a friend again. She picked out a couple of additional books and joined the checkout line.

Fortunately, the head librarian was reading to a group of toddlers. The bored teenager behind the desk checked Allie out and said, "That's a cool shirt." Nothing else.

It was a first for this town. Maybe things were improving.

MAURY would be leaving in a few minutes for football practice, and he was wielding the chef's knife in a rapid, rhythmic motion, chopping onions as if no one else in the world could get those onions chopped.

Mike watched him for a moment and saw he didn't look like his usual contented self. "Don't like chopping onions?"

Maury didn't turn around. "Sure I do. I like thin-slicing better, but chopping is fine."

Mike tried again. "You let a ball get past the line yesterday?"

"Nope."

Subtlety wasn't going to work, so Mike said, "Hey, something's wrong. The sooner you tell me what it is, the sooner we can fix it." He moved toward Maury and put his hands on the boy's shoulders, feeling the tension in his muscles.

"Something's happening around here," Maury said, "and I don't know what it is." He kept his eyes fixed on his work, and the knife chopped on steadily, as if it were on remote control.

Mike knew he had to be honest and open with this boy. "Well, I'll tell you what's happening, Maury. A company in New York wants to franchise the diner. You know, open some more like this one. Like the fast-food franchises."

"If that happens, everything will change, right?"

Mike knew he meant "everything will change for me." He was aware of Maury's background. His parents had moved from one place to another, looking for a job his father could succeed at, until one day his father gave in to despair and shot Maury's mother and then himself. However stoic, however oblivious to anything but cooking Maury pretended to be, he feared that the unexpected phone calls and the occasional worried expression on Mike's face meant his life was about to be turned upside down again.

It took Mike a split second to decide how to deal with Maury's worry. "I haven't decided what to do yet," he said cheerfully, "so relax for now. I'll keep you updated so you won't have any surprises."

Maury's chopping didn't slow down, but his shoulders seemed to lose some of their tension.

"If I do say yes, all it means as far as you're concerned is that after culinary school, I'm going to hire you before anybody else snaps you up. Whatever happens, you and

I are a team, okay? Where I go, you go with me as long as you want to."

Maury finally turned around. "That's what I want, to work where you do."

The simple statement touched Mike's heart. "I don't know what I'd do without you, that's for sure," he said. "Especially next Wednesday and Thursday nights, because that's when I'm going to New York to find out what these people are offering and tell them yes or no. Think you can hold down the fort here?"

Maury gazed at him with his St. Bernard eyes. "I'll handle it. What're the specials?"

"You tell me," Mike said, and in a few minutes they'd picked out dishes that were less labor-intensive than the ones he and Maury made together.

"How'd you like to make out the list of ingredients and place the order with the wholesaler?" Mike asked.

He watched the boy's face light up. "You think I can do that?"

"You bet," Mike said. He didn't care what Maury forgot, what he ordered too little or too much of. All that mattered was the look on his face. Now that Maury was okay again, he could go back to worrying about the lawyer.

Then it hit him that the only people he'd told about the franchise offer were his brothers, Barney and Maury. What that meant was that they'd become his family, and that felt good.

ALLIE LEFT the library feeling better. She had a few books to read, and maybe something in them would catch her interest. At least she'd taken a step toward planning her future.

She strolled aimlessly toward home, moving in a crisscross, taking her time, looking at the houses she knew so well, remembering good times—or bad ones— in most of them, the bad ones being dates to parties with the most repellent boys in school because nobody else would invite stuck-up Allie.

She hadn't been stuck-up. She'd been engaged in dreams of her future, dreams that lay beyond Serenity Valley.

And now she was back. So much for dreams.

She came to a street she'd always loved, the oldest one in town. Cottages sat close to the curb rather than set back, giving the impression of a village in the French countryside. A beautiful old Catholic church sat at the end of the cul-de-sac. A straight line of maple trees that the French-Canadians who'd settled in LaRocque had planted a hundred and fifty years ago shaded the houses.

Her favorite cottage was old Mrs. Langston's, which was coming up on the right. It was built of irregular stone and topped with a peaked roof of Vermont slate. An ancient wisteria vine draped over the front door and climbed to the roof, and clematis were staked up on each side of the house.

There it was, as charming as she'd remembered it. Allie took one glance and came to an abrupt halt. A For Sale sign stood on the tiny strip of lawn in front of the house.

Her heart sank. Was Mrs. Langston sick, too sick to stay in her house? Or even worse, had she died? That was surely something her mother would have told her.

As she stood there staring at the sign and worrying, a car pulled up to the curb. A couple in their sixties got out and came up to her, smiling.

The woman had been her first-grade teacher, Mrs. Langston's daughter. "Mrs. Appletree?" she said. "I'm so glad to see you."

"And you're—oh, my goodness," the woman said, "you're Allie Hendricks!" She gave Allie a hug. "I guess I've never stopped thinking of you as that serious little girl, all knees and elbows, who already knew how to read when you came to me." She turned to the man. "I'm sure you know Roger."

Who didn't? He was the state senator representing Serenity Valley. "Senator Appletree," she said, holding out her hand. "What a pleasure to see you again."

"Why, thank you, my dear," said the senator in his booming voice. "Would you like—" for a second, she thought he was about to offer her an autograph "—a tour of Mother Langston's house?"

Allie shook her head. "I love this house, but I'm not in a position to buy anything. I saw the sign and was worried about Mrs. Langston." She turned to Priscilla Appletree. "Is your mother—"

"We had to move her to assisted living," Priscilla said, shaking her head. "She *so* didn't want to go." Then she smiled. "Within an hour after she'd arrived she'd joined a bridge group and was already making friends."

"You're selling the house, I see."

"For a pittance." Priscilla sighed. "She'd gotten to the point that she couldn't keep up the maintenance. It's a real mess, needs painting, and it's stuffed to the gills with old papers and pictures. We're asking a lot less for it than we would if it were fixed up, but Roger and I stay so busy…"

"And Priscilla's dreading going through her mother's things," the senator said sympathetically.

"I'm sure," Allie said. "All those old memories. It's so hard to throw away any of them."

"Yes. Well, I'll have to do it someday, when we have a buyer." For a moment, Priscilla looked despondent. Then she said, "Let's talk about you. I heard you were back in town. Is anything wrong?"

"Nothing except my decision to go to med school," Allie said. "It just wasn't right for me. So I've come home to regroup, try something else when I know what it is."

"I know you'll make a good choice," Priscilla said gently, and patted her arm. "I, well, you know how small the valley is, and I did hear that your mother's not happy about your leaving school."

"It was a shock to her," Allie said, "but she's *trying* to understand, although I know she's still determined that I'll be a doctor. I feel so guilty about upsetting her, and I feel worse now that she's being so kind to me. Too kind." She smiled. "I feel like a four-year-old again."

"Mothers do that," Priscilla said. "Maybe it's time to leave home."

"I wish I could, but you don't make a lot of money going to med school." She forced a smile.

Roger and Priscilla exchanged a look, and Roger nodded. "Would you like to stay here for a while?" Priscilla asked her. "We could postpone the sale until I feel more like cleaning things up, repainting and that kind of thing."

Allie's mouth dropped open. "It would be like a dream come true. I've always loved this house. Um, it would depend on the rent, of course…"

"No rent," the senator said. "We couldn't rent it to anyone in its current condition."

It was too good to be true. "I'll clean it up," Allie said in a hurry. "I'll…"

"You'd better take a look at it, make sure you can stand even walking inside the way it is now."

"I can stand anything," Allie said fervently. "When could I move in?"

Priscilla laughed. "As far as I'm concerned," she said, "right this minute. I love your mother, but I know how determined she can be." Then she smiled. "Just like you, Allie Hendricks."

Allie realized that what Priscilla said was absolutely true. She and her mother were like two mules trying to share a stall. As she followed Mrs. Appletree inside, she felt like dancing. Her life was definitely taking a turn for the better.

MIKE HAD BEEN dreading the lawyer's call for two-thirds of the day, and now, looking at the last third, he felt he couldn't stand another minute of suspense. He'd overcooked one batch of flank steaks and Maury had rescued the next one just in time. Maury had snatched the sugar caster out of his hand when he'd picked it up instead of the sea-salt box, which didn't look anything like the sugar caster.

Each time the phone rang, he twitched. At last, he picked up the receiver to hear, "Mr. Foster? Earl Ritter here."

"Yes, Mr.—"

"I'm so sorry I'm just now calling. A family crisis and no cell phone, as my assistant told you."

"No problem," Mike lied.

"I'm afraid there is," Ritter said. "I'm sorry to be calling with some very bad news."

Mike felt his gut tighten. "Go ahead," he said.

"My client, Evan Howard, died yesterday morning."

Mike's hand froze on the receiver. Evan Howard had shaped his early life, had been the wall Mike had to break down to be the man he'd struggled to become. Now his nemesis was gone, just like that. It was over.

He should feel relieved. Instead, he felt deprived of the opportunity to prove himself to the man.

"How did he die?" he asked as calmly as he could.

Ritter sighed. "A dreadful car accident," he said. "His wife died with him. She was so young. It's such a tragedy."

Evan remarried? A young wife?

"The funeral is tomorrow and the reading of the will is on Friday. You'll need to be there."

"I wish I could, but I run a restaurant and have to be here. I want to send flowers, of course, if you'll tell me the name of the funeral home."

"Mike, you must be here." Ritter wasn't impolite, but he spoke so firmly that it took Mike aback.

"Evan wasn't really a close friend," Mike hedged, "so I, um…"

"He certainly thought of *you* as a close friend," Ritter said. "He's made you the guardian of his child, Brian Marshall Howard."

Chapter Four

Mike felt as if he'd been caught by a tide that was tugging him too far from shore to swim back. He needed to make some response to Ritter, but his mind had shut down.

"So you must be here, of course," Ritter repeated, "to take the appropriate legal steps before you can take charge of the child."

The tide released Mike for a second. If he didn't go, if he didn't take those appropriate legal steps, he didn't have to take charge of the child? It was a tempting thought.

But not an honorable one. "Of course. I understand. I need to make arrangements."

"Make them quickly. Celine's family is…"

Mike rubbed his forehead. A headache was building up rapidly. "Whose family?"

"You didn't know her? Celine is…was Evan's wife. Brian's mother." Ritter's voice tightened. "If you don't mind my asking, what exactly was your relationship to the deceased?"

If he told the truth, surely Ritter would understand that he had no idea how to be a good parent.

With his heart making a big lump in his throat, he said, "Evan Howard was my father."

Ritter's gasp hissed from the receiver. "He must have had a reason for not telling me he had a grown son."

Mike wasn't surprised to learn that his father had never mentioned him. "We've been estranged since I was sixteen. He couldn't possibly have wanted me to bring up his son."

"The will is quite clear," Ritter said stiffly. "I assumed he'd informed you."

Mike fell heavily onto one of the stools that flanked the big butcher-block table. "No," he said, "but I'll come to the funeral and the reading to see what's going on. Give me the details, where and when the funeral is—"

Ritter named a funeral home and its address, droned on about the time and whatnot, then said, "I *will* see you there." It was half question, half command.

"Yes." He had to do it. He had to find out what madness had overtaken his father to cause him to leave his child to Mike. Even without the background garbage, how could he raise his half-brother—good grief, he didn't even know how old the kid was—and run a restaurant? It was at least a sixteen-hour-a-day job, and when he slept, he dreamed about the diner.

Forget the restaurant, even. He hadn't the slightest idea how ordinary, caring parents, parents unlike the ones he'd had, raised a child.

The back door banged shut behind Maury, returning from football practice. "Maury," he said, "Barney, we've had a slight change in plans."

"What?" Daniel and Ian spoke in chorus.

"My father and his wife—number three, four, seven, I don't know—died in a car wreck and appointed me guardian of their son."

"How old is the boy?" Daniel asked.

"Did you know you had a half-brother?" came from Ian.

"In order, I don't know, and of course not."

"How can we help?" A typical reaction from Daniel.

"I don't know that, either, not yet." Everything was happening so quickly it was overwhelming. "I'm going to Boston tomorrow and coming back Friday afternoon. I've set up a plan for Maury and Barney. I'm pretty sure they can handle the diner for two days. I told Barney and Maury that a guy I went to culinary school with died in a tragic car accident, so you guys have to tell the same story."

"Sure," Ian said. "But what are you going to tell the boy? He needs to know you're his half-brother."

"Depends on how old he is," Mike said. "That's something I can think about later."

He was so distracted during the dinner hour he could hardly put on his "Hello, folks, glad to see you," face. Allie had shot him several curious looks. He didn't want to tell her or anybody else, so he'd avoided her all evening.

Finally he retreated to the kitchen and began getting things ready for Maury and Barney while he was gone.

He was worried about the diner, but deep down, he knew he didn't have to be. The last words Maury and Barney had said to him before the dinner customers began to arrive was, "Don't worry about anything," from Maury, and "Nobody's even going to miss you," from Barney.

He wasn't sure he didn't want anyone to miss him, but

their supportive attitude touched and cheered him. He was lost in thought when Allie moved up behind him.

"Guess we're about through for the night," she said. "Everything okay?"

"Sure is," he said.

He could tell she didn't believe him, but she said, "Good. Hey, guess what? I found a place to live today! It's absolutely perfect if you don't mind dust and clutter, and—" She interrupted herself with a sheepish laugh. "Sorry. I don't want to bore you with details."

"No, I want to hear about your house, but it turns out I have to go out of town tomorrow and I'm trying to do some prep work for Barney and Maury."

"Is there a problem?" She frowned, and her voice was filled with concern.

He knew why she was worried. It was a well-known fact that he never went out of town. He was always at the restaurant, downstairs in it or sleeping above it. "Sort of," he told her. "A guy I went to culinary school with died. He was a good friend back then. We lost touch, but I feel like I have to go to the funeral." He hated lying to Allie, but he had no choice at the moment.

"Of course you do." The kindness in her voice made the tension inside him ease a little bit. "I'm sorry, Mike. Even if he hasn't been a close friend through the years, I know you remember the good times you had with him then, and that has to make you sad."

It would if there'd been any good times to remember. "Thanks," he said. "I guess you're right."

"Maury and Barney will handle the restaurant all by themselves?"

"I hope." He hesitated, then said, "I know. I know they can handle it."

"If I can do anything to help them out, I will."

"They should be fine," Mike said. "Barney's been with me since we opened, so he knows the diner inside out. And if Maury wants to be a chef, he'd better find out early what a big responsibility it is."

"Call me if you need to talk to somebody, okay?" She scribbled on a scrap of butcher paper and handed it to him. "That's my cell. Sometimes these things affect us more than we think they will."

That shook him, too, the way things had been rattling him from the time he learned his father was dead. "Thanks again," he said, controlling the tightness in his throat. "I will."

And then with a sad, sweet smile, she said, "You'll be okay, Mike. I'll be thinking about you."

He nodded. "Thanks."

After Allie left, he spent a few more hours doing prep work that would make tomorrow and Friday easier for Maury and Barney. At one in the morning, he went upstairs to his apartment.

His entire life was in this small, two-hundred-year-old brick building on LaRocque's picture-postcard town square. Years ago, when Ian had found the valley and settled into Holman, and Daniel, still completing his veterinary training, had chosen to intern with the vet in Churchill, Mike was the lowest chef on the totem pole in a fancy restaurant in Boston. He was good, although it was hard to tell working under a demon chef who demanded perfection, but it would be years before he rose to sous chef, then at last, chef in some less well-known restaurant.

He wanted his own place, something less stressful. He hated to admit it, but he actually missed Ian and Daniel, however maddening they could be. More than that, he wanted to move to Serenity Valley. Life seemed so simple and peaceful there.

When the letter, written in a formal tone, arrived from his mother—how she'd found him he couldn't imagine—asking him to visit her in Burlington, he was reluctant to go. He hadn't been any closer to her than he had been to his father.

Still, he'd gone to see her, and found that she wanted to make peace with him. She'd finally understood why he'd turned into the petty criminal he'd been in his teen-aged years, understood that his father's and her neglect had contributed to his downfall.

He'd left feeling better about himself than he ever thought he could. He'd noticed how thin she was, but she'd always been thin, beautiful, sought after, the classic socialite, her involvement in "good works" stretching far beyond Burlington. He'd grown up in an elegant house, largely occupied only by him, his nanny and servants.

He'd had no idea she was sick until he received notice that she'd died, leaving a sizeable amount of money to "my good friend, Mike Foster."

The rest was history. Much too young to do anything grandiose, he'd bought the crumbling building, fixed it up, started his restaurant and made a success of it.

Now it seemed to be happening all over again, but this time, there would be no forgiveness, merely an inheritance that would turn his life upside down.

His senses honed by anxiety, he saw the apartment, where he'd lived from the beginning, when it was in shambles, through sharper eyes. It had been Allie who'd said, "You could make this place look so pretty," when he'd invited his skeleton staff upstairs for an impromptu party after an exhausting weekend.

Meaning, "How can you stand living in this hell-hole?"

The memory made him smile. He'd gotten the message. Allie and her mother—and he remembered her as a mother who adored her daughter—had volunteered to be his "decorators." They'd helped him produce a comfortable bachelor pad with leather-covered furniture and a large, worn Oriental rug, a bedroom and small office, a tiny, high-tech kitchen and a miniscule bathroom.

He was happy here. He couldn't imagine living anywhere else, living any other life. When he was ninety, he'd have an elevator chair installed in the wide staircase and sweep down to the kitchen to get things going in the morning.

What if he couldn't stay in the apartment with a half-brother to raise? His stomach muscles tightened again. It figured that his father, who'd done nothing but ignore him when he'd been young, was now messing up the comfortable life he'd made for himself.

In twenty-four hours he'd know. Feeling like a felon on death row, he packed quickly and, tired beyond belief, got a few hours of restless sleep. Long before the first rays of morning sun appeared, he was in the kitchen, waiting for Barney.

"What'd you do, stay up all night?" Barney asked when Mike showed him what he'd done the previous evening.

"Nope, didn't take me any time at all," Mike lied. "I just knew how busy you and Maury would be and wanted to help a little."

"We'll get along fine. I've been here so many years I know how to run this diner almost as well as you do," Barney said.

"I know, I know," Mike said, and sighed. "I'm just a little jumpy today."

"Losing somebody's never easy," Barney said, "even when you haven't seen that somebody in years. Goodbyes are tough."

Barney was an authority on that topic. He'd been devastated by his wife's death.

"Now go on and get out of here," Barney said. "It's gonna be a peaceful, ordinary day."

Mike only wished he could say the same thing about the day ahead of him.

MIKE HAD PROBABLY just left for Boston, and Allie was already missing him. She was sure it was because he was such a fixture in LaRocque, always there, that even a few days away left a gap only he could fill.

Her mother had been unusually understanding about Allie's wanting her own place. Allie thought, amused by the idea that maybe her mom was tired of waiting on her hand and foot. Early that morning, she'd moved into Mrs. Langston's house with two suitcases and a computer bag. Her worldly possessions.

Even though she was now living in squalor rather than in her mother's cozy, spotless house, filled with the scents of beeswax, lemon polish and baking brownies, she felt at peace. She sat in one of the velvet-covered wing chairs in the parlor, watching a cloud of dust rise as she squished into the cushion, and made a plan. She would have to clean. Buy groceries. Learn to cook a few things for herself.

Filled with purpose, she explored the closets and found a vacuum cleaner and plenty of supplies. She'd start in the kitchen, getting ready for her first cooking experience. She opened a kitchen cupboard. Yuck. Dust under and over the plates and glasses. She emptied the cupboard, cleaned it out thoroughly and ran water in the sink for washing its contents. With a stack of plates in her hands, ready to deposit them in the sink, she suddenly felt lonely.

How silly. She was thrilled to be alone after years of roommates, after two days of feeling guilty around her mother, wasn't she?

And she'd barely reinstated her friendship with Mike. Missing his presence in LaRocque, yes, but lonely for him? Absurd.

She had no intention of enduring the feeling until late afternoon when she'd start her shift at the diner. Examining her options, she decided that a person she wanted to get to know was Lilah Foster, and she really did have a number of questions about the benefit.

She looked up the number and dialed. "Lunch?" Lilah said, sounding rushed but delighted after Allie had introduced herself. "I'd love it. I need a break, too. You have no idea what it's like around here in the mornings."

"Oh, yes, I do," Allie said. "I babysat Daniel's kids once years ago. Just two days, but when it was over, I went home, put my feet up and didn't move for another two days."

Lilah laughed. "I'm amazed you survived at all. But back to the subject, lunch would be great. Let's see, where should we go?"

Allie actually giggled. Maybe she'd survive this low point in her life, too. "I hear great things about Mike's Diner," she said.

"No kidding. Okay, see you there—when? Straight-up noon?"

"Perfect."

It was early September, but the first frost had already

appeared on the pumpkins, so to speak, and the air was pleasantly crisp. Just as Allie reached for the door of the diner, a sparklingly pretty woman slipped up behind her, dressed in a blue turtleneck that matched her eyes. Allie held the door open, and the woman smiled. "Since I don't recognize you, you have to be Allie."

"Our minds were certainly running along the same lines," Allie said, following her into the warmth of the diner. "You must be Lilah. This is some town, right? To be able to recognize people by the process of elimination?"

Colleen bustled up to them, bearing menus. "Table by the windows?"

"Great. Thanks," Allie said.

"What's your favorite thing here?" Lilah studied the menu, although she, like Allie, must have memorized it.

"The chocolate meringue pie," Allie confessed, "but I guess I have to address the major food groups first."

"Not necessarily." Lilah gave her a mischievous look. "I'm discreet."

"Unfortunately," Allie said, "I'm hungry enough to have both."

"Me, too," Lilah said, settling back with a deep sigh. "It's bad enough now. When school starts next week, by the time I've done the get-off-to-school-do-you-have-your-homework-lunch-money routine, I'll feel as if I'd built a barn with my own two hands."

"Omigosh," Allie said, "that time I babysat, I didn't ask about lunch money."

"I strongly doubt anybody starved," Lilah said, and then added, "although the population at our house shifts constantly, so for all I know, some poor, starved boy wandered the wilderness for years eating fruits and berries, a pathetic bag of bones before—"

"Before Daniel found him and gave him his lunch money," Allie said. She really liked Lilah.

"Exactly," Lilah said, "so back to favorite things, I'm almost evangelistic about the grilled cheese with bacon and tomato, and my absolute favorite dessert is the coconut layer cake, so whatever you order, I'll match you calorie for calorie."

"The grilled cheese is my thing, too," Allie said.

"We're soul sisters. I knew it."

Colleen appeared, not looking at all harried in spite of the fact that customers waited at the door, others had a finger lifted for more coffee, dessert, their check. "What'll we have here?"

They gave her their order. "How're things going?" Allie whispered to Colleen, "without Mike."

"We don't even miss him," Colleen said as if she were reading from cue cards, then dashed to the kitchen like a rabbit on wheels.

"She's lying," Allie said. "They miss him."

"I bet it killed him to leave," Lilah said. "He was pretty sad last night. I could tell when he called."

"I'm sure he was. The funeral of an old friend is always difficult."

"Not that Mike would come right out with his feelings. You know how he is."

Allie wasn't at all sure she knew Mike. Or Mike's brothers Daniel and Ian. She'd always sensed something secretive about them. They were so different. Mike with his reddish-brown hair and green eyes, Daniel so blond, and Ian, dark inside and out. More than that, their personalities were equally different, Mike so gregarious and funny, Ian so brooding, Daniel so sweet and caring.

For some reason, she suspected there was more to Mike's attending the funeral than met the eye, but she didn't know Lilah well enough to say so. Instead, she changed the subject. "I'm already having a good time working on the benefit," she told Lilah. "Mike's dreamed up a terrific menu, surprise, surprise, and I'm working on a color scheme." She reached into her handbag and brought out a folder. "I want it to be just perfect. Here are some samples…"

Throughout the lunch, she and Lilah discussed details and specifics of the fundraiser, but they also had fun. Lilah was easy to talk to and had a wicked sense of humor.

When she said goodbye, Allie felt happy. Her move back to the valley was shaping up nicely. She had a salary coming in, a place to stay, and a volunteer job for as worthwhile a cause as there could possibly be.

ON HIS WAY to Boston, Mike observed the rules of the road, knowing he was tired and upset. During the entire trip, he brooded over the reasons his father might have had for writing this bizarre clause in his will, leaving his son in Mike's care. It didn't make any sense.

Driving in Boston didn't leave much room for thought. He navigated rotaries, one-way streets and sardine-can traffic and at last made it to the funeral home where his father would be honored. Remembered, anyway. Mike couldn't wait to see if anyone honored the old man.

After he parked in an overpriced garage, he put on his suit jacket and, properly somber-looking, entered the Sisters of Light Chapel of Rest prepared for anything except the possibility of missing a good night's sleep at the Boston Inn, where he'd booked a room at a price that staggered him.

He resented every dollar he'd spent on this trip, obeying the last command of a father who'd disowned him. His mother's dollars had opened the diner. She, at least, had realized at last that he wasn't the bad seed, just a kid too long neglected, a kid who'd been given his freedom too early, before he'd had time to sort out what that freedom could do for him in a positive way.

So freedom and reckless behavior had been one and the same to him until the night he stole his father's car and crashed it through the plate-glass window of a local shop, and for the first time in his history of petty crimes, his father didn't bail him out. That's when he went to the correctional facility, which was the best thing that had ever happened to him, because he'd met Ian and Daniel there.

He entered the chapel, then halted when he saw the two closed caskets. Evan Howard had lived a life Mike knew nothing about. Maybe he'd changed. Maybe this new wife had been a gracious, warm and loving woman who'd convinced his father to forgive his prodigal son.

He'd never know.

He recognized no one at the funeral, but he hadn't expected to. He sat down in an inconspicuous spot and waited for the mourners Evan Howard and his new wife had thought of as family to fill the front rows.

No one filed in. No family? No one else, no one who understood what a normal family was like, who would welcome Brian into their happy home?

The chapel was full, though. Business associates, almost certainly. Friends, probably. Bouquets packed the dais, topping and surrounding the coffins. A group of young women sat together, some of them crying. Friends of Celine's?

The service began. The minister pontificated for a while about what a wonderful wife, mother and daughter Celine had been...

So where were Celine's parents? They ought to be fighting him for the guardianship of her child.

...and what a wonderful man Evan Howard had been. He actually said, "a fine man and a great humanitarian."

One of the group of young women went to the podium to say what a wonderful friend Celine had been.

Two friends of Evan's rose to say what a wonderful member of the community he had been, probably disappointed that the minister had already said, "a fine man and a great humanitarian."

Both Celine and Evan had apparently been wonderful. During speeches from more business friends and golf buddies, Mike resisted the impulse to doze. At last it was over. Someone at the funeral had been Evan's lawyer, but Mike didn't stick around to find out who. He needed some serious sleep.

ALLIE WAS halfway down the block from the restaurant, still thinking what an open, friendly person Lilah was, when she realized she'd forgotten the folder containing the linen samples and her notes on the benefit dinner. She turned back and found herself wondering how Mike was doing. Losing an old friend could hurt, but funerals could also be stark reminders of one's own short time on earth. When she reached the diner, she went directly to the table by the windows where she and Lilah had sat. The bright-red folder was gone.

No, it wasn't. Colleen stood at the pass-through into the kitchen waving it at her.

Allie smiled and started toward her, but Colleen pointed to the counter and raced on to her duties.

She picked up the folder, and stayed a second to say hello to Barney and Maury. "Whoo," she heard Barney say. "Everybody's eating lunch today. I'm wiped out. I feel like an elephant's sitting on my chest."

It was the word *chest* that galvanized her into action. She darted toward the swinging door to the kitchen. She found Maury, wide-eyed, still holding his chef's knife, staring at Barney, an unfamiliar Barney, whose face was gray and pinched.

She rushed toward Barney, with Maury right behind her. "Are you all right, Barney?" she asked calmly.

Instead of answering, he slumped to the floor.

"I'll call 911," Maury said in a scared, shaky voice, and Allie knelt beside Barney, checking vital signs with no equipment except her fingertips.

MIKE WENT straight to the hotel, checked in, lay down on the bed and slept for two hours.

He woke up hungry, called room service—to hell with the cost—and ordered a bacon cheeseburger with all the trimmings—to hell with gourmet food. While he waited for it, he decided to call the restaurant, because even in his worst moments, he couldn't say "to hell with the restaurant."

"Mike's Diner," said a lovely, familiar voice.

"Allie?" His heart thudded.

"Oh, Mike, I'm so sorry you called."

"Well, thanks. Give it to me straight. What's happened?"

She sighed. "Nothing for you to worry about until you get back."

Mike froze, worry creeping up his spine. "What don't I have to worry about until I get back."

"Well, Barney had a—a spell of some sort and had to go to the hospital."

"He had a heart attack, didn't he?" Mike rested his head on his hands. He'd known Barney had been working too hard and hadn't done a thing to stop him. Barney meant so much more to him than great burgers. He'd been like the father Mike had never had.

"He'll be okay. Colleen's holding the fort at the hospital and calling in with the news, Becky's taken over the grill and the griddle, Maury's filling the other orders and I'm waiting tables. We'll have reinforcements by tomorrow morning."

"I'm coming back. I'll be there in—"

"No," she said with a firmness that surprised him. "It looks as if you stayed up all night making things easy for Maury and Barney. Stay right there, and we'll see you tomorrow night."

He wanted to argue with her, but he did have the guardianship to deal with. He needed to get this bump in his life leveled as soon as possible. Reluctantly, he agreed to monitor the situation by phone. Room service arrived, he ate dinner with a glass of wine, then stretched out on the bed and was asleep within five minutes.

"MIKE?" Ritter stepped into the hallway, held out a hand and gave Mike a solemn look that he probably meant to be comforting. When Mike nodded, Ritter said, "Before we go in, I wanted you to know that Celine's parents would be here to meet you, but it seems tragedy begat tragedy. Her father had a cranial bleed soon after hearing the bad news, and even if he lives, her mother will have a full-time job taking care of him."

So no parents, no grandparents. This kid wouldn't have anybody but Mike.

Feeling even more weighed down by responsibility, Mike followed Ritter into the conference room. A handful of people were already seated around an oval walnut table, and a few more drifted in. Representatives of charities Evan had supported? Devoted household help?

A middle-aged woman, attractive but bitter-looking, joined the group. An ex-wife, maybe?

"We're all here now," Ritter said ponderously as he opened a document and began to read.

He read Celine's will first. It was short and boilerplate, with no mention of her child. Next, Evan's will. Gifts to several charities, as Mike had surmised. There were gifts to the devoted household help, most of whom cried when they heard the news. The bitter-looking woman had inherited a sum of money that made Mike's head reel, probably a condition of their divorce.

Then Ritter cleared his throat. " 'In the event that a minor child or children of whom I am the father should survive both my death and their mother's, I appoint Mike Foster, currently residing at—' " and his address and phone number followed " '—as the guardian of that child or children and also appoint said Mike Foster as trustee of any trust funds of said child or children, to be used at said Mike Foster's discretion.' "

So that was it. Without falling in love, without a mutual agreement with a wife to have a child, Mike had one, a child with trust funds.

The rest of the morning went by in a blur of signing

papers and at last, the trip with Ritter to the Howard house to pick up Brian Marshall Howard and take him home to LaRocque.

The "minor child" wasn't a sad young boy. He was an eight-month-old baby.

Already panicked, Mike couldn't breathe. He wouldn't be like a big brother to this infant, he'd be like a father! What did he know about being a father?

Brian was half-asleep when the nanny—of course his father and Celine would have had a nanny—handed him over. Terrified, Mike peered down at the baby's peaceful face, and Brian opened his eyes to gaze up at him.

They were green. Carroty red hair like Mike had when he was a child. Pale skin, the kind that freckled.

He looked just like Mike.

Chapter Five

Mike parked his car behind the diner and shut off the engine. His nerves were shot. For what seemed like the thousandth time, he took a look at Brian.

His brother. His *baby*.

Throughout the trip, Mike had been afraid the baby would start crying, missing his parents, his nanny. Then, inexplicably, he'd find himself worrying when Brian was quiet for too long. Should he stop the car and check on him?

It had been a harrowing experience.

In the end, the kid had slept most of the trip, safe and sound in his car seat, which Mike thought could easily protect an astronaut during a launch, unaware of how much anxiety he was causing the man driving the car. He woke up once, making noises that did sound like the prelude to an all-out crying jag. In a panic, Mike had pulled into a rest area. One bottle and a clean diaper later, the upheaval had been resolved.

But now that the car had stopped moving, Brian was showing signs of waking. What a terrifying thought.

Mike should have gone across the river to Daniel's house and asked—no, begged—Daniel and Lilah to rescue him. Pride had stopped him. Stupid, useless pride. He hadn't wanted to look weak, look like this was something he couldn't handle. He'd been handling his own life since he'd been a teenager. A baby wasn't going to throw him for a loop. At least, he hoped not.

Daniel and Lilah would be thrilled about Brian. Ian would give him that dark brooding look that said, "How in hell are you going to do this?"

Maury didn't know Mike was bringing home a baby. He was already worried about the changes franchising would bring about. How would he feel about Brian? Talk about a major change.

Mike got out of the car and went around to the side door. When he opened it, Brian opened his eyes and took a look at his surroundings. Then he took a good look at Mike.

His eyes were big and round, but he didn't look scared. Not knowing what else to do, Mike waved at him. Brian started waving his arms, too, and making burbling noises. Mike figured he'd better take him inside. Sooner or later, he had to face the music. The whole town was going to go crazy when they learned what had happened—a highly abridged version of what had happened.

He undid the many straps that held Brian in his car seat and picked him up. Brian settled immediately on Mike's left hip.

"Okay, Brian," he said on the way to the door, "I don't know how many times you've been out in public, but we have to talk about certain matters of etiquette. Smile at everybody. It's good business. No crying. No, um, bodily fluids on anybody's clothes. Got it?"

Brian smiled at him. Even though he knew the baby didn't understand what he was saying, it looked as if he intended to cooperate.

When he reached the back door of the diner, he pulled

a deep breath into his lungs for fortification, and then went inside. His heart sank when he saw a thin older man standing at the grill and realized it wasn't Barney, but a stranger. Two more strangers were roaming around, too. But Maury was at the stove and Allie stood at the counter assembling salads. Looking at her, Mike's knees seemed to melt.

"Is the spaghetti about ready?" Allie was calling out to Maury, but when she turned toward Maury, she saw him.

"Mike! Welcome—" then she saw Brian "—home," she said on a gasp. She came directly to him—well, not to him but to Brian. "Who is this?" She gazed up at Mike, obviously stunned.

No more stunned than he was.

And no one had ever looked more stunned than Maury.

They'd noticed, both of them, the uncanny resemblance of this baby to him. He had to distract them. "I should have called ahead, but things happened too fast," he said, looking straight at Maury. "My friend, the one whose funeral I went to, well, he left me a little something in his will and this is the little something. Someone, I should say." He tried to sound amused, but failed.

"Oh, Mike," Allie said, "he's adorable." Shocked or not, she seemed absolutely delighted that he'd brought home this human present from Boston. "What's his name?"

"Brian."

Maury still stood at the grill. He studied the baby for a moment, and then said to Mike, "He looks like you."

No point in trying to distract them now. It was only

a matter of time before everybody noticed. "Amazing, isn't it? Well, my friend looked a lot like me, too. People would ask if we were brothers." Mike held his breath until he saw that Maury and Allie seemed satisfied with his answer.

Maury turned back to his work. "What will you do with him?"

Mike knew what the real question was—how will this interloper change things?

"I was asked to raise him. I'm his guardian, so I have to raise him. Somehow." Almost as if he didn't like the way Mike had explained the situation, Brian reached up and gave Mike's collar a hard tug.

Allie saw it and smiled. "Well, it's nice to meet you, Brian." She did a mock curtsey, and for the first time in hours, Mike felt some of his tension ease.

He shifted Brian higher on his hip. "How's Barney?"

Allie's mouth twisted wryly. "Resting comfortably and doing as well as can be expected. That's all the hospital staff will tell us."

Mike sighed. "I'll visit him as soon as I can. How are things going without him?"

She couldn't seem to take her eyes off Brian. "Fine," she said absentmindedly. "Becky is helping out in the kitchen and Colleen is covering out front," Allie told him. "A few of their relatives," she waved vaguely around the room, "have pitched in, too."

"I appreciate what everybody's done, and I'll hire temporary help as soon as I…" Now that he had a baby to take care of, when would he find time to hire staff?

Allie stroked Brian's cheek, and he gurgled appreciatively. "He's so calm, when this has to be a major upheaval in his life."

Mike looked down at Brian, who was examining the kitchen with bright, curious eyes. He was so small, so helpless. The tightness returned to Mike's shoulders.

How was he going to take care of this child?

His panic increased when the back door swung open and Lilah, Daniel and Ian all peered through it. "We *had* to see him," Lilah said.

"This is terrific," Daniel said.

Ian raised his eyebrows.

Just the reactions Mike had predicted.

"What a precious baby," Lilah said, rushing toward Brian with her arms outstretched.

"Well, let's see who we're adding to the family," Daniel said easily. He lifted Brian off Mike's hip. Mike stretched to the right, getting his balance back. What a relief.

"I want to hold him," Lilah begged.

"Me, too," Allie challenged her. "I saw him first."

"Wait your turn, ladies," Daniel said. "Hey, Brian," he said, and Mike saw that Brian was smiling at Daniel and reaching out for his hair. "Meet the rest of your family. This is Maury," and he went straight to the boy. "Maury is your new dad's very best friend and right-hand man. You want to get on his good side."

Mike saw Maury turn slowly from his chopping. "Hi, Brian," he said awkwardly. Brian chuckled and reached out for Maury's arm.

"I'm Uncle Daniel," Daniel went on, "and this is Aunt Lilah."

Brian gazed carefully at each face, as if there'd be a test later.

"You've met Allie, and this is Uncle Ian." With a big smile, Daniel held the baby out to Ian, who accepted him with a look of horror and held him at a distance. "Hey," Ian said, "you like sheep?"

"My turn to hold him," Allie said swiftly as she rescued both Brian and Ian.

"Darn, you're fast," Lilah grumbled. "How can we help you settle in?" she asked Mike.

He'd been watching Allie tickle Brian's stomach, giggling along with him. "I have a bunch of his things in the car. They're shipping a lot more. Man, I had no idea babies required so much stuff. *I* don't have that much stuff."

Lilah firmly removed Brian from Allie and started her own game with him, peek-a-boo. "Your brothers can unload the car, and you can figure out where to put all that *stuff*."

Mike gave Allie a helpless look, and she laughed. "I'll give them a hand," she said. "I'm no good in the kitchen, anyway."

Boy, it was good to be home. The last two days had been unnerving, and the only thing that had gotten him through them had been the knowledge that soon he'd be home, surrounded by family and friends.

Backup, that's what he needed. With some help, it would all work out.

WHEN A desperate summons from the kitchen sent Allie racing downstairs to wait tables, Daniel, Ian and Lilah surrounded Mike.

"He looks a lot like you," Ian said. "Too much."

"I noticed," Mike said grimly. "Maury noticed. Everybody will notice. That'll get the gossip going."

"We'll deal with that later," Daniel said, sounding more crisp than usual. "Why would your father have left you his child to raise?"

Mike sank onto a box of books and held his chin in his hands. "I've been trying to figure it out. I don't think he really meant for me to raise him," he said. "He didn't know he and Brian's mother were going to die."

"Then why did he do it?" Ian persisted.

"All I can think of," Mike said slowly, "is that he got a kick out of imagining me, twenty-five years from now, sitting in a lawyer's office with my tongue hanging out, hoping for a big inheritance, and finding out he'd left me nothing."

"But as you said, he didn't know he was going to die," Lilah argued, looking up from a box of clothes. "You'd have to like and trust someone implicitly to leave your child to him."

"Oh, please," Mike said. He suddenly felt so tired, more tired than he could ever remember being. The adrenaline that had gotten him through the last two days and safely home with Brian was all used up.

"It's getting late. If you'll help me figure out how to get Brian through one night, I'll start organizing for real tomorrow morning after the breakfast rush. I need to visit Barney—" He halted. "I can't visit Barney. I have a baby."

Lilah patted him on the arm. "I'll keep Brian for you while you see Barney. He's doing fine, by the way. All he needs is a lot of rest before he comes back to work."

"I'll go to the grocery store," Daniel said, checking his watch. "He came equipped with everything except food."

"Anything for him to sleep in?"

"A sleeper with feet, yes. But he do͏͏ crib."

"We have a crib in the attic," Daniel sai͏

"I'll take care of that," Ian said. "Any shee͏

"He has sheets," Lilah said. "Baby-blue linen. *Beautifully ironed.*"

Mike's brothers groaned along with him.

"Go see Barney," Daniel said. "We'll have you all set up in a couple of hours."

Mike sent his gaze toward each of them. "How am I going to do this?" He whispered the words.

"Nothing to it," Daniel said, smiled at him and ran down the stairs.

"GET OUTTA HERE and go run the restaurant."

"Hello to you, too," Mike said, and smiled at Barney.

It was hard for him to smile. Barney might be doing "as well as could be expected," but he sure didn't look good. Too quiet lying there in the sterile hospital room, nothing like the whirling dervish he was in the diner kitchen. His skin was gray, and his eyelids drooped. Seeing him this way was like having a knife stabbed into his heart, but he couldn't let Barney know he was upset.

Hiding his feelings, he sat in a chair next to the bed and got into a relaxed position. "Doctors say you're doing great."

"I know I'm doing great," Barney said. "What I want to know is when I can go back to work."

"Pretty soon," Mike said easily. "When you're well. Don't worry, I'm hiring some temporary people when I can get around to it. Your job will be waiting for you."

"Who's doing it now?" He actually sounded ~~us.~~

"Maury's at the grill, and some people I don't know are helping out. Thank God I hired Allie."

"Nice girl. Just like her mom."

Mike noticed that Barney's gruff voice had softened a little. But everybody had a soft spot for Allie.

He was wondering whether to tell Barney about Brian. He didn't want to bring on another heart attack, but on the other hand, he didn't want Barney hearing it from anybody else. "Um, I have a surprise for you, well, a surprise for everybody."

"Boston baked beans?" Barney said hopefully.

"I have a baby."

Barney looked at him with such shock that for a second Mike wondered if he should call a nurse. "A baby? A baby what? Dog? Cat?"

"Human," Mike said, then recited once again his story about his old friend and his unexpected inheritance.

"Well, I'll be," Barney said. "A baby." To Mike's surprise, he actually smiled. "That'll perk things up."

"To say the least." Mike felt relieved.

"How's Maury taking it?"

"Okay. He's a great kid." He hoped it was true.

"Well, good." Barney gave Mike a sly grin. "I hope you're taking it the same way."

His smile faded, and he suddenly looked so tired that Mike realized even this short conversation had worn the old guy out. He said his goodbyes, and as he stepped out the door, Elaine Hendricks stepped in, carrying a bouquet of flowers. "Elaine, good to see you."

"Allie told me about Barney," she said, looking embarrassed. "I know how busy you all are at the diner, so I decided to check on him and sit with him awhile."

"That's very kind of you," Mike said.

"Oh, he's asleep," she whispered. "Maybe I…"

"No, I'm not," Barney said, sounding as if just saying the words was an effort. "Just resting my eyes."

Mike left them there together. Elaine Hendricks was a kind woman. She'd be kind to Allie whatever Allie decided to do. He was sure of it.

At home he found Daniel and Lilah on the floor with Brian crawling back and forth between them. They'd wrecked his tiny office to put a crib into it. Baby things were strewn everywhere. "Okay, the reinforcements have arrived," he told them. "You two get home to your own kids."

"Are you sure you can handle it?" Lilah asked.

"Of course he can," Daniel said. "We'll show you a couple of things…"

Thirty minutes later Mike was a trained father. A father figure, that's what he was. But trained was one thing. Being a good father figure was a whole different thing. And he didn't even know where to start.

"WANT TO SEE a restaurant in action?" Mike asked Brian when they were alone.

Brian yawned deeply.

"Bedtime soon," Mike told him, "but D-Dad," he stumbled over the word, "has to go to work for a few minutes first." He heaved himself up off the sofa and took Brian downstairs.

Five minutes later, he realized he'd made a terrible decision. First, Colleen and Becky zeroed in on Brian, and Allie, who was plating desserts, had to pry them away to deliver the last orders of the evening.

Allie herself looked as if she'd like *him* to put desserts on plates so she could hold Brian. It sounded like a good idea to him, too, so he handed the baby over to her, glanced at the order slips and started slicing the cherry pie. And what did she do? She took Brian out into the restaurant to show him off.

From the pass-through, he heard her telling his lie to the regulars, that a friend who coincidentally looked just like him had left him a baby. They neglected their perfectly cooked—he hoped—properly hot—he hoped—dishes to play kissy-face with Brian.

The lie circled around him like a shark waiting for him to make just one mistake. Brian's resemblance to him didn't go unnoticed, and he saw a few quizzical looks exchanged among the women.

He also saw he'd just cut up a whole cherry pie and put the wedges on plates. He checked the order and saw that everybody at the table had ordered something different.

"Oh, shoot," he muttered. He'd had a baby for one day, and he was already falling apart. He stalked out into the restaurant and took Brian away from Allie. "Your shift in the kitchen," he told her, smiling for the customers' benefit, and for her ears only, "and please do something with all that cherry pie."

MIKE WAS EXHAUSTED, but not too exhausted to get up a dozen times in the night to see if Brian was still breathing. On Saturday morning at five, he heard gurgles and coos coming from what had once been his office and was now Brian's room. Once upon a time, as in two days ago before he went to Boston, he could wake up at five-thirty and still be in the kitchen by six. Those days were over.

Mike changed Brian, washed him off—he needed a lesson before he attempted a full bath—and after examining the supply of baby food, decided that cereal was a logical starting point. He held Brian on his lap to feed him. He'd need one of those chairs kids sat in to eat, but Brian seemed perfectly happy on his lap, gobbled down his cereal and was delighted by the pureed apricots straight from the jar.

Curious, Mike tasted them. They weren't bad, although, personally, he might have added a pinch of mace, an eighth of a teaspoon of cinnamon. Or maybe a touch of grated fresh ginger.

After he'd fed his new baby and washed him off—again—and changed his diaper—again, he dressed him in the outfit Lilah had laid out—an overall kind of thing embroidered with seriously cute ducks and a yellow turtleneck to put under it. He had no place to put Brian while he showered, shaved and dressed except the crib. Brian complained, his babbling sounding cross and impatient, and Mike couldn't blame him. He understood, oh, wow, did he ever understand, the frustration of being ignored. They had to have some kind of chair, or swing, something Brian could sit in and watch Mike shave.

Down to the restaurant they went. Weekend mornings were the busiest, and Maury was already there, preparing for the rush. Allie was at the stove getting a head start on the homefries.

Mike took a look at the homefries. Not your usual Mike's Diner breakfast potatoes. Black here and there… but you can't look a gift horse in the mouth. If you lost a few customers, so what.

"Ah," she said brightly. "You both made it through the night alive."

Colleen and Becky arrived with a couple of the strangers he'd seen last night, then the first wave of customers. Toast burned and over-easy eggs turned into hard-cooked ones while they all, even Maury, left their jobs to engage Brian in conversation. At last Mike grabbed a sausage, wrapped a pancake around it, moved himself and Brian to the corner of the room farthest away from the action and directed things from there.

This situation had to change, too. But how?

First, he had to hire temporary help. Real, experienced help. But before or after he bought equipment for Brian? Depressed, he ate his makeshift breakfast, then checked on his customers.

Everyone who'd come to dinner the night before had told everyone who might come to breakfast this morning about the baby, so he had to go out and make the rounds. Nobody complained about the eggs, the potatoes or the cold biscuits. Every customer was smiling—at Brian, who rewarded them with gurgles, waves and occasional dives at their plates.

Of course, Brian didn't understand the lifted eyebrows, the knowing looks, the sidelong glances among the diners that went along with the smiles and coos. Mike was glad that at least they were able to separate the two issues. Brian was perfect even if he might possibly be Mike's illegitimate child.

The breakfast crowd didn't dissipate until almost eleven, much later than on weekdays, and he took Brian back upstairs while his motley crew cleaned up and got to work on lunch. Glumly he surveyed the boxes and bags, the piles of unpacked clothing and toys stuffed into every nook and cranny of his apartment. It was a nightmare come true.

He'd barely had time to change Brian's diaper—was it normal to be wet as often as Brian seemed to be?—when his whole family descended on him.

"You still need a high chair and lots of other baby equipment," Lilah announced. "Are they shipping any of those things from Boston?"

"His furniture looked like a store display," Mike said. "I told the lawyer not to bother. I'll need to buy all that stuff."

Lilah took Brian from him. Mike would have liked to think he wasn't relieved, but he was. Getting used to being a parent was not a piece of cake.

"I'd like to help with the shopping," she went on, "but I've got my hands full with the kids today," she said. "Give Allie time off to go with you."

"Hey, he doesn't need a woman to help him buy for this kid," Ian protested.

Lilah laughed. "I wasn't being sexist, just practical. I heard that Allie's been helping out in the church's daycare since she was twelve and was everybody's favorite babysitter. She probably knows a few things about babies." She looked pointedly at Mike. "Do you?"

She had him, and they all knew it. He looked at Daniel, his brother with the most knowledge of children.

Before he could even start to ask, Daniel laughed. "No way. I've got patients three deep at the clinic."

Mike glanced at Ian, who said, "You've got to be kidding."

"I hate to bother Allie again," Mike said. "She's already taken on too much since Barney's attack."

"Maybe you should pay her," Ian muttered.

"I am paying her. You think I'd ask her to work for free?"

"No, pay her for helping with Brian. You know, like a nanny."

"That's a separate topic," Mike said. "We were talking about baby equipment."

"Just looking ahead," Ian said. "You're going to need help."

"Ask her," Lilah said. "She might say no, but you can always ask."

"I'll ask her if she'll help me shop, but I'm not going to ask her to be a nanny."

At the very moment he needed Daniel's mediation tactics, Daniel was digging through the toys, frowning when he found one that had a lot of small pieces.

Ian shrugged and started going through a box of books. He held up one of them. "While you're shopping, get the kid some books besides leather-bound gift sets of *Kidnapped* and *Treasure Island*."

"And clothes," Lilah called out from Mike's bedroom, where she'd gone to change Brian.

"You brought up four boxes of clothes last night," Mike protested.

"Right, and most of them have to be ironed. Or dry-cleaned." She emerged from the bedroom with Brian, whom she'd changed into navy trousers and a wool sweater.

Mike blew out a sigh. He needed help. Lots of it. So maybe asking Allie to go shopping with him was an imposition, but it would be just one afternoon. "Okay, I'll ask her," he said, more to himself than to anyone else in the room.

"Of course you will." Ian stood up and started down the stairs.

Mike frowned. Was Ian going to ask her himself? Or bring her up here?

Lilah handed Brian back to Mike. "I have to go, and so does Daniel. But we're as close as the phone if you have an emergency."

What was she talking about? His whole life was an emergency.

"I appreciate what you've already done," he said,

leaning his head away from Brian, who'd latched on to his earlobes, "more than I can tell you." Good thing the kid was so cute.

Ian shoved open the front door. "Here she is."

An obviously confused Allie followed him into the small living room. Her gaze landed on Mike and Brian.

"Ian said you needed to talk to me immediately."

Mike shot Ian a frown, which his brother ignored, then back at Allie. "Um…I was wondering…I mean if you wouldn't mind…could you—"

"The man needs a nanny," Ian said bluntly. "He wants you. He'll pay big bucks. Okay?"

"Ian!"

Ian just shrugged at the chorus of voices. "Needs to be said."

"I was only going to ask her to go shopping," Mike said, really irritated at Ian. But at the same time, he suddenly saw himself in the kitchen *without* Brian on his left hip, saw himself cooking with both hands while Brian was up here in the apartment, happily playing with Allie. The thought was nearly irresistible.

He looked back at her. She'd gone completely still, her eyes round and unfocused. He felt an edge of anger, not at her because she was going to say no, but at himself for wishing she'd say yes.

THE VOICE in Allie's head was her mother's. "Allie, you'll get attached to that baby and you won't want to go back to school." Realizing everyone was staring at her, she finally found her own voice.

"You can't imagine how much I'd like to take care of Brian," she said slowly. Her eyes dropped to the floor. She couldn't look at any of them, especially Mike. "But

I'll only be here until January, and I'm supposed to be doing whatever it takes to decide on a new course of education."

"Of course," Mike said swiftly. "You can't take on a full-time job, especially one that…that…"

"That takes so much emotional energy," Lilah said quietly. "I'm sorry. We weren't thinking."

Now Allie could face Mike. "I hope you can understand. Maybe I could help in some other ways, like keeping him out of the way in the restaurant, and I know a lot about babies from all those years of taking care of them at church, so I could offer you advice…" She trailed off. Mike was giving her an embarrassed smile.

"All advice welcomed," he said.

To Allie's relief, the room came to life again, the three brothers talking about Barney and hiring more help, Lilah making funny faces at Brian and saying, "We could easily keep him for you from five to ten, Mike…"

Allie felt tears welling up. "I'm sorry," she said one more time. "I guess I'd better get back to work." And she fled down the stairs.

She felt horrible, but she'd done what she had to do. "You'll settle right back into the valley," her mother had said. "You'll be a waitress the rest of your life."

Or a nanny for the next twelve years. She knew herself too well. Establish an emotional attachment to Brian, and she'd never leave.

And then there was the fact that Brian looked enough like Mike that they could be father and son. No. She wouldn't think about that. It was impossible.

At the foot of the stairs, she paused. The restaurant wasn't all that busy. They didn't really need her.

She went back up the stairs, where Mike looked surprised to see her. "I could help for a few minutes right now," she told him. "I could take Brian for a walk."

"He doesn't walk yet," Mike said.

Allie gave him a "how dumb can you get" look. "In a stroller," she said.

Mike looked at Lilah. "He doesn't have a stroller."

The way the whole crew fell silent and began to stare at her made Allie nervous. After a long moment, Lilah said, "If you wouldn't mind going with Mike to Baby Heaven in Rutland this afternoon, he could outfit Brian a lot faster."

"Lilah…" Mike said in a warning tone.

"Sure." Allie smiled, feeling much better. "I'd be happy to do that. What about two o'clock, when the diner quiets down? You'd be back in time for dinner."

"I can't," Mike protested. "I have pot-au-feu to cook."

"You don't have a stroller," Ian said. "Or a high chair or that thing you were talking about, a chair that rocks and rolls, or whatever, so Brian can watch you shave."

"For a man who was scared to hold a baby, you're all of a sudden an expert?"

"Time out," Daniel said. "If you don't get the stuff you need, the next few days will be a nightmare. So figure out something simpler for dinner, and then go shopping."

Allie waited for the verdict.

"Okay," Mike said, looking like a man sentenced to death, "I guess that's what I have to do. After I check in on Barney."

"How DOES he look today?" Allie asked Mike when he joined her in the hospital lobby after he'd spent a few minutes with Barney.

Mike sighed, worry etched on his face. "Better. More color in his face. He just needs to take it easy for a while. Which isn't what he wants to do. Hey, Brian, did you shake up the place while I was gone?" He held out his arms for the baby.

"He was an angel," Allie said. "He smiled and waved at everybody who walked by. He's a real charmer." He *was* charming, and warm and soft while she'd held him in her arms. She steeled herself against falling in love with him.

"This was Barney's wakeup call," she told Mike. "He'll have to change his lifestyle, get some exercise…"

Mike simply nodded as they went to the car. Agreeing with her? Or not interested in what she had to say? And why should she even care? At the moment, she was along for the ride, a bizarre ride with an unprepared father to a baby warehouse.

It was so unreal that she didn't dare analyze it. Best just to do it and examine her motives later.

On the drive to Rutland, Mike's cell phone rang. "Steve," he exclaimed. "Speak of the devil. I was going to call you tomorrow." As he listened, Allie saw his face brighten. "You couldn't have asked at a better time," he said finally. "Send them down, the sooner the better. I've been saved," he told Allie. "The Vermont culinary school needs a couple of spots for their second-year students to have hands-on experience."

"What great luck." He sounded so excited it made her smile. "You'll make it, Mike," Allie said. "You and the restaurant both will get through it with five stars."

He fell silent for a while. Allie considered drawing

him out, but decided it was best to leave him alone. The man had been through so much in the past few days. He'd lost a friend, brought home a baby and had his right-hand man felled by a heart attack. That kind of stress would get to anyone. If the story of the friend's bequest wasn't true, he was under even more stress. She couldn't believe Mike would lie, but in a situation like the one she was imagining...

Baby Heaven was a huge warehouse-type store that was guaranteed to carry everything any child could need. Mike looked shell-shocked when they got inside.

"Where do we start?" he said.

"Clothes. What's our budget?"

"Nearly infinite," Mike said. "If I run out of money, this kid's rich. My friend left him a ton of money in trust. I can draw on it if I need to, but I'm planning not to need to."

"Your friend must have been very successful in the restaurant business."

He gave her a blank look. It only lasted a second or two before he said, "Yeah, I guess he was. Okay, let's get going."

There *was* more to Brian's story than Mike had told her.

Again she felt the lump of worry growing in her stomach. It would hurt to know that Mike had fathered a child with another woman. Why it would hurt so much she wasn't sure. But it would hurt worse to know that Mike hadn't brought the woman home, helped her get the child off to a good start in life. It would shake her faith in a man she'd thought of as responsible, caring, even heroic.

Maybe there were other reasons. She was a wealthy

woman who didn't want to marry a small-town restaurateur…

Baby clothes, she told herself firmly. We're shopping, not speculating.

The clothing aisles were splashed with color. She and Mike wandered around for some time before she found what they needed. She selected a few outfits, then Mike added a few more. When she glanced at him, he shrugged. "He's been changed twice today already. No matter how much we buy, it won't be enough."

When Allie laughed, Brian joined in, smiling and bouncing in the shopping-cart seat. He looked at Mike, then raised his arms, the universal sign that he wanted to be held, and Mike complied, picking up Brian and settling him on his hip.

"You know, I think Brian loves you already," she said.

Mike stopped in his tracks. For a moment, he looked down at Brian, and then he looked at Allie. A flash of all the confusion and stress he must be feeling flitted across his face, only to disappear and be replaced by his usual smile.

"I think he just wants to see better."

"Sure," Allie said, and then, when Brian immediately started grabbing at all those colors, added, "Hmm. Maybe you're right."

Two aisles over, they found the strollers. Allie suggested one. Mike pushed it back and forth a few times and said, "Fine."

Next they went to the crib-bedding shelves. Allie stood back and let the guys handle this one on their own. She couldn't remember ever seeing anything as interesting as Mike and Brian picking out crib sheets.

She didn't bother to point out to Mike that Brian was too young to understand what they were doing.

The pair gave their choices thorough consideration. When Mike held up sheets covered with fast racing cars, Brian giggled and bounced with great excitement. Allie realized the baby was reacting to the excitement in Mike's voice and the vivid primary colors of the cars, but still, you could imagine the two of them were having a conversation.

"Yeah? These?" Mike studied the sheets, then pronounced, "Good choice, buddy." He walked over to Allie and tossed the package of sheets into the cart. "He likes cars."

She bit back a smile. "Was there ever a man who didn't?"

As Mike and Brian headed down the next aisle toward bouncing, rocking baby chairs, something Mike seemed fixed on, she spied a display of stuffed animals and spent a few minutes squishing them before she picked out a rabbit she couldn't resist and tossed it into the cart.

When she caught up with Mike and Brian, she paused just to look at them for a minute. Watching Mike with Brian was really getting to her. He was kind and patient with the baby, and she admired the way he'd taken on this responsibility.

If she wasn't careful, Brian wasn't the only one she was going to fall for.

Chapter Six

Brian snoozed happily in his crib, but Mike felt unsettled. Restlessly he paced the apartment, always pausing at Brian's open door to listen to his breathing.

He knew a glass of good wine or a simple over-the-counter pain reliever would help him relax enough to sleep, but he didn't know if a new father was allowed to drink even one glass of wine or take even one pain reliever until his child was old enough to scream, "I have pneumonia!"

In the path of his pacing, he saw a purple folder buried in a towering stack of papers. They had once been in his office-now-Brian's-bedroom and Allie had moved them onto a bookshelf in order to make space on his desk for the equipment Brian would need.

He pulled out the folder. It was his Abernathy file. He'd almost forgotten about his trip to New York. How could he honor the commitment he'd made to Richard Stein?

His first thought was the money Abernathy had spent in order to get him to New York: drivers, plane tickets, hotel and more. So he had to go.

His next thought was what to do about Brian. There he drew a blank.

If he called Daniel, he'd get the full You-can't-go

routine. So he called Ian, who stayed up late, and not because he had a baby whose breathing had to be monitored.

He reached a wide-awake Ian and explained the situation. Ian's analysis, because Ian was the analytical one of the three of them, shocked him.

"He just lost his parents—and his nanny. You're all he has. You can't leave him this soon."

"He gets along great with Allie. Maybe she'd keep him—just this one time, of course."

"You and he need to bond."

Bond? Where had Ian learned about bonding? And what exactly did it mean?

"So to bond with him, you'd have to take him to New York," Ian went on, "You've just moved him to a new place. If you take him to New York, you're taking him to another new place, also the wrong thing to do."

Mike was suddenly irritated, depressed, he didn't know which. "I thought I could count on you for unbiased advice, but you're sounding just like Daniel."

"Because that's the kind of thing that happened to you and Daniel and me," Ian snapped.

His words hit Mike right in the gut. He'd never felt close to his parents. Daniel had felt only fear and loathing for his father. Ian's mother had bonded with a liquor bottle, not with him.

"I see your point." He heard Ian's whoosh of breath. "I'll cancel the trip. And, Ian, thanks."

He left the folder on top of the stack to deal with first thing in the morning, then checked on Brian again. He'd never go to sleep now. He gave up, turned on the lamp in Brian's bedroom—its base was a bright-red Mini Cooper—and settled into the biggest rocking chair for sale at Baby Heaven, and still not quite big enough.

Brian made him nervous. No, *nervous* was too mild a word. Brian scared him to death. He knew nothing about babies. Heck, he didn't really know much about kids. Sure he hung around with Daniel's foster kids, but those boys were older.

Brian couldn't talk, couldn't walk and, most importantly, couldn't tell Mike when something was wrong or if he was in pain. Mike would have to figure it out all by himself.

Fortunately, he had the information at hand. He opened the baby-care book Allie had insisted he buy. "A user manual?" he'd quipped when she put it firmly into his shopping cart. In fact, it was just what he needed. The book was helping him understand more about Brian. What stage he'd reached, what he needed from Mike, and what Mike could expect in the near future.

The book had a short section on the fear new parents felt. Mike thought that part should have been much longer. He'd never been the type to give up on anything, but Brian hadn't been one of his goals. A baby had been thrust on him, a complete surprise, a global change in his life.

He wondered again why his father had left Brian to him. Lilah's he-trusted-you theory was pure Lilah, kind and positive, but he didn't believe it for a second. Mike would stick with his own hypothesis, that his father had thought this day would never come, that Brian would be an adult before Evan died, that Celine would outlive him by thirty years, so he'd thought of it as a joke. A cruel joke.

Well, the day *had* come. Brian was entirely dependent on Mike. And Mike would *not* be like his father. But how? He had so much to learn.

Brian made a murmuring sound. Mike was on his

feet in an instant, adrenaline racing through his body like fire. When he leaned over the crib, Brian moaned. Mike reached out and touched his forehead.

Hot. The baby felt hot.

It was not the time to look up *fever* in the baby book. He had touched Brian only a couple of hours ago, and he'd felt cool and normal. Now he was hot, and he was waking up.

Forcing himself to stay calm, Mike went to the bathroom and got the basket of medical supplies Allie had put together. Inside was a thermometer, the kind you stuck in the baby's ear. He went back to the room and now Brian was whimpering. "It's okay, buddy," he said, trying not to let his anxiety show. Carefully, he took Brian's temperature, and then he freaked. A hundred-two.

He wrapped Brian in his comforter and went for the door, his mind on autopilot. On the way down the outside steps to his car, he grabbed his cell phone out of his pocket and called Allie. When she answered, her voice groggy with sleep, he immediately blurted out, "Something's wrong. Brian's sick. I'm on my way to the hospital with him."

He didn't wait for her answer, her calm voice, her reassurance. He couldn't. Talking was the last thing he could do at the moment.

He was too consumed with fear.

ALLIE PARKED in the hospital's parking lot near the E.R. and sprinted inside. When she reached the waiting room, she saw Mike immediately. He was holding a fussy Brian, and he looked desperate.

"Hi," she said, sitting next to him. "How's Brian?"

"They haven't seen him yet." Mike sighed. "I'm sorry I called you. I wasn't thinking."

"I'm glad you called me." Allie leaned over and ran her hand gently over Brian's forehead. Mike was right. He had a fever.

"He'll be fine," she said.

Mike nodded, but tension oozed from him. Brian was sitting in his lap, his head against Mike's chest. Mike kept rubbing the baby's back and murmuring soft words. For a man who didn't know a thing about babies, he was doing a great job.

They waited another twenty minutes before a nurse called Brian's name. Mike stood up, started forward, then looked back at her. He seemed surprised, but grateful, when he saw she was following him. The nurse led them into the back section of the E.R. to a small room with two chairs and a bed. Mike put Brian on the bed and held him there, and Allie stood on the other side to help if she needed to.

The nurse asked Mike what Brian's symptoms were. Then she weighed the baby and took his temperature. Brian cried softly during the exam, settling down only when the nurse left and Mike once again held him.

"He's even hotter than he was at home," Mike said flatly. "I don't know what happened."

Allie patted his arm. "Try not to worry," she said soothingly. "It wasn't anything you did wrong. And I'm sure it'll turn out to be nothing serious. Babies' temperatures go up higher than adults' when they're sick."

Mike didn't seem convinced, but he didn't say anything. While they waited, Allie studied the room. It was a standard E.R. examination room. Although the hospital was fairly small, it was well-equipped.

She'd wondered if being in a hospital would make

her nostalgic for med school. Instead, she felt relieved. She wasn't certain what path was right for her in life, but she knew in her heart she couldn't handle a baby in pain, wasn't meant to come into this room in a white coat or green scrubs and deliver bad news to frightened parents.

A few minutes later, the doctor walked in. She was a young woman with a wide smile. "What an angel," she said, looking at Brian, then at Mike. "He's the spitting image of you," she marveled.

"He has a fever," Mike said rapidly. "And I think he's in pain."

The doctor read Brian's chart, and then examined him. It didn't take her long to find the problem—an ear infection.

"It happens sometimes at this age," she told them, writing in Brian's chart. "I'll give you a prescription, and the nurse will tell you how to bring down his fever."

"He won't lose his hearing?" Mike asked.

The doctor smiled. "Nope. In a couple of days, take him to his regular doctor to check his progress."

After the doctor left, a nurse came in and handed Mike a prescription for antibiotics. Then she gave Brian a dose of acetaminophen, walked them through how to bring down the fever with lukewarm baths and sent them home.

"You two have been up all night," she said sympathetically. "I hope you can get some rest tomorrow. Or today, I should say."

Of course she assumed they were Brian's parents. It made Allie feel uneasy—but, somehow, good.

When they reached the parking lot, Allie turned to Mike. "I'll wake up Cliff Hemphill and tell him you need this prescription filled in a hurry."

"Wake him up?"

"Happens to him all the time," Allie said. "Either let people wake you up, or run a twenty-four-hour pharmacy. While I get the medicine, you can take Brian home and give him his lukewarm bath."

For a minute, she thought Mike was going to protest. He looked at Brian for a moment, then said, "Okay. Thanks." He sighed. "At least a chef knows what lukewarm water is." He turned his gaze on her. "I'm sorry for dragging you into this. I didn't know what to do," he said.

She could see how rattled he was. "You did just the right thing," she said. "I'll see you back at your place."

Mike gently strapped the fussing baby into the car seat. "Thanks," he said. "You're too good to me." With a rueful smile, he added, "Be careful, or I might get used to it."

She knew he was teasing, but after he'd made the statement, his smile faded and his gaze held hers.

Allie found herself holding her breath as a tingling awareness feathered across her skin. Then Brian began to cry, and the spell was broken.

"Have to get him home," Mike said, looking away. "I'll leave the doors unlocked."

Allie nodded. She'd known Mike for years, but suddenly, things were changing between them. From his expression she was fairly certain Mike wasn't too happy about the changes.

But she'd be lying if she said she wasn't.

WHAT COULD possibly have made him call Allie? He couldn't say, "made him *decide* to call Allie," because he hadn't even thought about it. He'd just called.

Driving slowly home, Brian snuffling in his car seat, Mike chewed his lower lip. Daniel would have come in an instant, would have driven Mike and Brian to the hospital, would have stayed until the situation was under control. He had a houseful of boys who must have gotten sick at some time or other.

Instead, he'd called Allie.

Maybe she'd been on his mind because they'd spent the afternoon cleaning out Baby Heaven. Or maybe she'd just been on his mind. That moment in the hospital parking lot—that had scared him.

In the back seat, Brian's snuffles escalated to wails. "We'll be home in a minute," Mike said soothingly, feeling that he wanted to call the baby something like "sweetheart," or "angel."

Yep, he was losing it. Big-time.

THE PHARMACIST had come cheerfully to the rescue, wearing jeans and a pajama top. Allie got back to Mike's apartment with the medicine to find Mike holding Brian, sitting in the white rocker lulling him to sleep. He overwhelmed the rocker, looking like a man sitting in a child's chair. His vivid eyes gazed up at her, and he whispered, "He's stopped crying, and his temperature's down to a hundred already."

"How are you holding up?"

"Resting comfortably and doing as well as can be expected," he said, twisting his mouth into a wry smile as he remembered her saying the same thing about Barney. "How about you?"

"I pulled lots of all-nighters in med school. I'm a pro. How will you get through tomorrow? Today, actually."

"Ask me tonight."

Allie cleared her throat. "Brian should stay up here today, not necessarily in bed, but he needs rest, not excitement."

He looked startled by the idea. "I don't know how I can arrange that. I have to be downstairs, and I'm sure not going to leave him alone."

"I was thinking," she said hesitantly, because she *had* been thinking—thinking she was about to do the wrong thing, "that if the crew could do without me, I could stay with him today. Just this once."

"You shouldn't be using your time that way," Mike said.

"I'd be doing it instead of waiting tables," she insisted. "While he naps, I'll rest."

"I don't…"

"What are your options? It's time for you to go downstairs right now. It's too early to call babysitters. I don't mind, really."

Mike's face was a study in conflicting feelings. "It's very kind of you to offer," he said, "and you're right, I need help immediately. I might be able to find somebody else by noon…"

"Don't worry about that yet," Allie told him. Her own insides were full of conflicting feelings. "Let's give him his first dose of medicine, then you get ready for work. We'll be fine."

While they gave Brian his medicine, Mike's hands occasionally brushed hers, and each time she felt a spark of new life in her tired body. She had to concentrate on Brian, keep her mind off her surprising reaction to Mike's slightest touch.

"Look at him," Allie said, smoothing Brian's damp, curly hair back from his forehead. "He's sound asleep."

He was, his head buried under Mike's chin, his fingers clutching Mike's collar, his knees drawn up with Mike's arm around them to keep him close. The image of the two of them touched her somewhere down deep in a place she was afraid to go.

"Think I could get him into bed without waking him up?"

"If you can turn a turkey on its side in a hot oven, you can get him into bed." She smiled at him, and it seemed to increase his confidence.

She admitted to herself how glad she was that he'd called on her to help, that she was here with him. Now he looked calm, ready to see Brian through this glitch in his otherwise healthy state.

Mike stood slowly and carried Brian, still snuggled up, to his crib. She joined him and leaned over the crib railings. "He's the most beautiful child," she whispered. "He looks—"

She turned to gaze up at Mike, not wanting to see the remarkable resemblance of man to child but forcing herself to confront it. What she confronted were his eyes, and something in them turned her to jelly, pushing her doubts down deep inside her. He lowered his mouth to hers and brushed it softly. She felt more than a spark, a jolt of electricity as their lips met, then a sense of falling through space when he deepened the kiss. She responded to it with all her heart and soul, and when he raised his arms, she knew he would put them around her to hold her close.

Instead, he pushed himself away. "I'm sorry," he said, making distance between them. "It's been an emotional night. I didn't mean to…"

Her eyes felt heavy. Her mouth felt swollen, even

though his touch had been so light, and much too brief. "For me, too," she said softly.

"I have to shower and get down to the kitchen," he said in a hurry, continuing to back away. "Do you mind if I—"

"Close the nursery door and I'll sit here with Brian while you dress," she said, but just now, she couldn't take her eyes off him.

He gave her one last, confused look. When the door closed behind him, she collapsed into the rocker. Her whole body zinged with pleasure. She wrapped her arms around herself and wished they were Mike's arms holding her tight against his chest, the length of his body.

The shower ran, and she shivered, imagining him soaping himself, picturing the water running over his muscular body. She ached with longing.

She wanted him. It came as a shock to her. She was in the grip of full-blown desire. And she wanted to believe the kiss had been a sign from him that he was seeing her differently—and liking what he saw.

Or was it just a sign of appreciation from a frightened new father?

She heard a soft knock on the door, got up and opened it to see Mike holding out a cup of coffee. How long had she been daydreaming? He was dressed and smelling of something nice and woodsy—and standing as far away from her as his arm could reach.

Yum. Aloud, she said, "Manna from heaven. Thank you from the bottom of my heart."

He shrugged awkwardly. "I'll come up when things slow down to see how he's doing," he said, "but if there's any change for the worse, call me immediately."

"Okay." She let her eyes drift over him for a moment, but he looked away. "Cream and sugar in the kitchen," he said, "and somebody will bring cinnamon rolls as soon as they're out of the oven." He gave her a shy, sidelong glance. "Then eggs and bacon and some of those biscuits."

And with that romantic announcement, he skittered down the stairs.

Allie leaned against the doorjamb. She liked her coffee with cream, and her men sweet.

WHAT HAD HE DONE? Just as he'd thought he'd gotten through his first big crisis, he'd gone and kissed Allie.

And he was very much afraid she'd liked it.

He didn't have time to do right by a kid. He sure didn't have time for a relationship with a woman, because he was supposed to be bonding with the kid.

And if he grew really attached to her...

She'd leave the valley to get established in her career. He *couldn't* leave the valley. He had the restaurant, and now he had a baby who needed to put down roots.

So he'd screwed up once, but he wouldn't again. He and Allie could be friends, but that was all.

Oddly depressed by the thought, he started preheating the big ovens and the grill.

He missed Barney like he'd miss an arm.

Why, oh, why had he let himself kiss Allie?

Dear Lord, he had a baby to raise.

As these thoughts rambled through his head, he realized he was sweating like a longshoreman.

He'd almost suggested she nap on his bed, but the thought of Allie lying on his bed had sent a flash of sensation to his groin, as it was doing now.

He had to get off this dangerous, winding road. Mountains rising to the right, and a sheer drop on the left. A barrier in one direction, a dive into despair on the other. They had totally different, totally incompatible goals. She was going out in the world. He was staying right here in LaRocque.

All alone, he sent up a cry of pain. "Ah-h-h," he yelled, just as Mildred Witherington walked through the back door with two pans of unbaked cinnamon rolls ready for their last rising and trip to the oven. The pans she'd expertly balanced tipped, and he dashed forward to rescue them.

"What's the matter with you this morning?" she said crossly. "I'm only fifteen minutes early, and I've been walking through that door with something or other for four years." She glared at him. "When do I get to meet that baby? The town's talking about nothing else."

He didn't like the way she said it, that the town was talking. Mildred had been his pastry chef since he'd decided he couldn't handle that job and everything else. She was well-known as the town's best cook. She lived three doors away from the restaurant and she delivered eight pies, four cakes and now, forty-eight cinnamon rolls every day, walking them over as soon as they were ready, and seemed to enjoy it in her own glum, uncooperative way. On the other side of the coin, she was the worst gossip in town, and he had a bad feeling that the gossip was, once again, about him. And Brian.

Mike said, "What's wrong with me is that Brian got an ear infection and I've been up all night. You can meet Brian as soon as he's well."

"Oh, the poor little thing," Mildred crooned. "Earaches are so painful. If it would help, I could come over and bake the cinnamon rolls."

Babies seemed to change everybody's personalities. "Thanks," Mike said hastily, "but I'll have plenty of help in just a few minutes."

"Well, all right," Mildred said. "I have to run. I have cake layers baking."

And phone calls to make.

Mike just had time to breathe a sigh of relief before Maury stepped in. After they'd said their hellos, Mike said, "Who were all those people in the kitchen when I got home?"

"Well, Colleen's Uncle Fred was on the grill, but he wasn't that great, so I'm on the grill now and he does toast and waffles. Becky's daughter plates the food and Colleen and Becky wait tables like always."

"So we've hired two extra people."

"No, that's just breakfast."

"Enough!" Mike said. "I get the picture, and I'm grateful to everybody who's helping, especially you, for pulling it all together."

Maury blushed and ducked his head.

Mike's smile faded. "This baby, Maury, is more trouble than you could ever imagine. Thank the lord for Allie. Brian got sick last night and she's taking care of him today."

"That's what I thought when Barney keeled over," Maury admitted. "That I was glad Allie was here."

Mike gazed at him. "It was scary, wasn't it?"

"Yeah," Maury muttered and turned away, getting ready to cook breakfasts to order.

Mike's heart went out to him. His own childhood was nothing compared to Maury's. The boy would wear those scars the rest of his life even though Daniel had given him a safe, dependable environment, and the worst thing that could happen to him now was that he'd scorch a pan. But the past must have folded in on him, the terror, the feelings of helplessness, when Barney'd had his attack.

And next, Mike had brought Brian home.

"How's he doing this morning?"

Maury had read his mind. He was trying to handle the matter of Brian gracefully, but it had to be hurting him. He still stood with his back to Mike, working away at the breakfast prep, and Mike went over to give him a hand.

"His fever came down right away, so I think he's better. I tell you, son, when he got sick it nearly scared me to death. It turned out to be an ear infection. I guess babies get them all the time, but I didn't know that. You can guess what a jerk I felt like. Somebody makes me the guardian of his child—biggest responsibility in the world, Maury—and right off, I screw it up."

"No, you didn't," Maury said, looking straight at him now. "You don't know what it's like to have parents who screw up."

The pain and anger in his face, the tension in his body, made Mike so sad that he said without thinking, "Yes, I do. Not like yours did, but it left me hurting inside just like you."

"But you're happy now."

"It took time."

Maury's brow furrowed in thought, making him look more like an English bulldog than a St. Bernard. "Daniel and Uncle Ian had the same parents. Why didn't they end up hurting inside?"

Yes, Maury thought slowly, but at times like this, much too well. Mike knew he had to answer the question, and he had to answer it honestly. "They did. We all got over it in time."

"How much time?"

"The time it took us to grow up, educate ourselves

and find professions we liked. Seems like you've already done that. You're a lucky guy."

Colleen, the wiry man who had to be her Uncle Fred, Becky and Becky's daughter rushed through the back door. "We're late," Becky gasped. "My son brought the car home on fumes last night and we had to get gas."

As she spoke, Mike heard a less-than-discreet knock at the door of the diner and everybody went into action. He raced to the door and said, "Gosh, I'm sorry. I forgot to unlock it." Behind him he heard the clatter of silverware as Becky and her daughter hurried to set the tables. The scent of coffee filled the air along with the smells of bacon and sausage Maury had just flung on the grill.

The day had begun. Just an ordinary day, except that upstairs he had a sick baby—and an all-too-enticing babysitter.

Chapter Seven

Mike stared at the phone in the kitchen, reached out for it, drew back, gritted his teeth and reached out again. He had to call Richard Stein and tell him he couldn't come to New York Wednesday, and he was dreading it.

He also knew that when you dread something, the best thing to do is to get it over with.

He took the receiver and Stein's number outside, pulled in a deep breath of the cool fall air, then dialed.

Stein was on the line swiftly with a hearty, "Mike! Good to hear from you!"

"It's not good news," Mike said.

"Oh?" Stein's voice was filled with concern, even anxiety. "What's the problem?"

Mike had thought carefully what to tell the man, and had decided to tell the truth, or almost the truth. "I inherited a baby." He'd made it a mantra, that *I have a baby* line, hoping one day he could say it without feeling shocked.

"You—" Stein sounded nonplussed.

"Yes. An old friend died and appointed me guardian of his eight-month-old child."

"Wow. That's, well, a real change in your life." Stein seemed to be gathering himself together.

"I'm supposed to stick with him for a while until he gets to know me, and the family tells me he ought to stay right here until he feels at home. So I won't be able to come to New York this week."

Mike waited for Stein to say, New York style, "So fuhgiddaboutid," meaning forget about franchising the diner, but instead, he was murmuring, "Of course, of course."

Mike rushed on to the hard part. "I feel bad about you having to cancel all the arrangements, and I want you to know I'll be happy to pay for the expenses you've already incurred."

"Nonsense, Mike! The expense is no problem. Of course you have to bond with your little one."

Even Stein knew about bonding.

"I'll keep in touch," Stein said heartily. "When you think it's okay for him to travel, let us know, and by all means, bring him along."

With enormous relief, Mike disconnected the call. All done, no conflict, no recriminations.

He sauntered back into the kitchen, a new man. "I don't have to leave town Wednesday," he said cheerfully.

In the midst of a chorus of "thank goodness" from the rest of his staff, Maury just gave him a look. When the kitchen emptied out, the boy said, "You're not going to franchise?"

"I have to think about it some more. I *will* talk to them in New York sometime, just to hear what they have to say. And I'll tell you all about it."

At ten he slipped out of the kitchen and ran upstairs to check on Brian and Allie. They were both asleep, but Allie's eyes popped open as soon as he walked into the room, and she instantly rolled off the sofa and darted into Brian's room. Mike joined her. "Relax," he whispered when he'd pressed his hand lightly to Brian's forehead. "He feels cool. Has he been in any pain?"

"No, and he'd let me know if he had been. It's about time for another dose of medicine, but I thought I'd wait until he woke up all by himself."

Mike gazed at her. Her hair, usually as smooth as a raven's wing, was mussed, and her eyes drooped with sleepiness. She looked beautiful. "Go back to sleep," he said. "I can stay a while. I'll take care of him when he wakes up."

"Nope," she said firmly, forcing her eyes wide open, "you have a job to do. We'll be fine."

He sighed. "Promise to call if you need help?"

"I promise. Breakfast was wonderful, incidentally. It's good to be the chef's babysitter." She smiled at him, and her sleepy eyes began to sparkle.

She was wide awake now. He took one more look at her, hoping his longing didn't show, and went back to the kitchen.

ALLIE PACED the room, physically agitated and yes, tired. And worried.

She worried about the new passion she was feeling for Mike and the motherly feelings she'd had for Brian from the first time she held him in her arms. Her mother had warned her about getting too comfortable in the valley and deciding to stay, and Allie could *not* let that happen.

She wanted a career as badly as her mother wanted one for her. Career opportunities were slim to none in the valley. So, as she'd told Mike, whatever career she chose, she'd have to be prepared to move, and perhaps move again. To be a desirable candidate for a job, she'd have to be unencumbered. It would be different when she was firmly established in her chosen field, but not until then.

Then there was the uncertainty about Brian's parentage. Realizing she was wringing her hands, and that she didn't want Brian waking up to a distracted babysitter, she decided busywork was the thing to do. She put a load of Brian's laundry into Mike's apartment-sized washing machine, then dived into one of the bags from Baby Heaven and started cutting off price tags.

MIKE WOKE UP thinking about the nightmare yesterday had been. He'd checked on Allie and Brian twice more, but when he went up to tell her he was home for good and she could leave, she looked exhausted.

Even exhausted she was cheerful. "We had a wonderful day," she assured him. "He needs to keep taking his medicine until it's all gone, but he's acting like a well baby. He's asleep, clean and should sleep through the night."

"What a relief," Mike said, and yawned. "Are you awake enough to drive home?"

"Do you have to be awake to drive in LaRocque?" She gave him that mischievous smile.

"Just be careful."

"I will," she said more seriously. "See you in the morning." She hesitated. "I'll come in my waitress uniform, okay? But if I'd be more helpful staying up here with Brian, then..."

"Thanks." He wished he could have thought of something more eloquent, but he couldn't.

He'd checked on Brian and undressed himself, started to get into bed naked, as he usually did, then realized he wasn't alone anymore and needed to observe a few modesty rules. Was there anything about his life that wasn't going to change? He picked out a pair of boxers, the green ones printed with apples. He should probably buy some pajamas, maybe a robe. Or was that going overboard? He pulled up the boxers, checked on Brian one more time, left a light on in his room, slid into bed and fell asleep at once.

But not for good. It must have had to do with rem cycles, because every two hours he woke up, got out of bed and made the short trip to Brian's room.

On the way back from one of these trips, he realized that if he told Allie, or Daniel and Lilah, maybe even Ian about his night runs, they'd assume he was driven by love for his baby brother. They'd be wrong. What drove him was a sense of responsibility, something he hadn't learned at home, but from being brothers with Daniel and Ian.

"I CAN ONLY stay a minute," Mike told Barney when he dropped by for a visit the next day between breakfast and lunch. "Everybody's getting less of me right now." He sighed.

"What've you done with Brian?" Barney asked him. "Shut him in the pantry with cans to stack? Couldn't be that. We don't cook outa cans."

Barney actually did look better today, which made Mike feel better. "He's being handed from Colleen to Becky to Allie to Maury—he's crazy about Maury, for some reason. Think about it, Barney. The diner's going to hell."

"It's worth it," Barney cackled.

That was the last thing Mike would have expected Barney to say. It opened up something inside him, made him want to tell Barney what he'd been thinking about last night. "I know. He's a great kid. I want to do my best for him, and one thing I do know is that a parent's supposed to love his child." He paused for a moment, wondering how to explain. "Well, what I'm feeling isn't love. It's sheer terror of not being able to meet the awesome responsibility of bringing him up right."

"I felt that way, too, when my oldest boy was born. Like he was a new dress Midge had sprung on me, with the bill to boot. Like I had nothing to do with it. Just like you're feeling now. Love comes later. Takes time. When they smile at you. When they say 'dada.' When they act like they'd like you to hold them. Stupid, ay-uh? But it happens." He sent Mike the closest thing to a smile Barney was capable of.

Barney was, on the outside, the least sentimental person he could imagine. If Barney could feel that kind of love, maybe he could. Time and a couple of "dada" moments would turn Mike into the kind of parent Brian should have. He hoped so, but parenting was more than love and a sense of responsibility. He just wished he knew what the rest of it was. Brian was such a cute, funny, happy kid. He deserved a dad who knew.

He repeated the words in his mind, cute, funny, happy… Brian didn't act like a neglected child. Had his father changed? He'd been in his mid-sixties. Had time mellowed him? Relaxed him? Calmed his workaholic nature? So that Brian might have had a father who played with him, cuddled him, talked to him, all the things Mike had never had? Or had Brian simply had a loving mother and a really great nanny?

If his father had changed, it hadn't happened in time for Mike. Leaving Brian to him in the event of his death had been his last blow, and his most cruel.

"Barney," he said, "I wish you'd been my father."

SINCE BARNEY'S heart attack, Allie had been doing double, triple duty at the diner. The chefs in training would arrive tomorrow, and the situation should improve. Brian was doing fine, and Mike was back in full force, but still she'd arrived early.

Arrived first, in fact. She'd expected Mike to be there, but he wasn't, so she turned on the lights, and as she was wondering what to do next, Maury dashed in, started the ovens and the grill and got to work.

She began setting tables. While she was laying out silverware, she heard a sound unlike any other in her experience, a deafening clang as if a thousand steel rods had hit the ground all at once.

Rushing outside, she saw that next door, just in front of the three-story historic building that was scheduled for restoration, someone had, indeed, dropped a thousand steel rods onto the ground.

Maybe not a thousand, but a lot. She waved at the truck driver and the men with him, and her heart stopped pounding. Scaffolding, of course, so that the workmen could painstakingly replace the original crumbling mortar between the bricks and replace broken slate tiles on the roof.

When the reverberations from the rods died down, she heard screams coming from Mike's apartment. Darting into the foyer at the foot of the stairs, she almost ran into Mike, disheveled, barefooted and harried-looking, with Brian in his arms, wailing.

"What the hell was that?" Mike's teeth were clenched together.

"Language," she said, then tried to explain over Brian's screams. At last she pointed out the foyer window.

"Scared the—daylights out of him," Mike said.

She could only read his lips. "Do you think his ears could be hurting again?" she asked him, pulling on her own ears.

"He was just fine until the moon fell to earth," Mike said loudly. "I have to get dressed for work. I don't know what to do."

At the moment, he was rubbing Brian's back, trying to cuddle him at the same time he was fighting off punches from Brian's fists.

"Okay," Allie said, reaching for the baby, "go back upstairs and toss his coat and hat downstairs. Then get dressed while I take him for a walk. Maybe that'll settle him down."

Mike gave her a grateful look and fled. Allie waited at the foot of the stairs, deafened by Brian's screams in the tiny space, until she was pelted by Brian's outdoor gear and the diaper bag, followed by a leather jacket and gloves that must be for her. Allie flung on the coat, no time to think how sweet that was of Mike. Dressing Brian was like dressing an enraged cat, but she managed at last and got the stroller onto the sidewalk with Brian in it, twisting in his seat.

She tried showing him the steel rods, explaining they were the source of the noise, but wasn't surprised when that didn't work. So she set off with him at a swift pace. Motion might put him back to sleep. At just that moment, the workmen began to move the rods, and Brian went into high gear.

She began to sing. He screamed louder, if that were possible. Lights went on in the houses on the square. Curtains twitched. Allie gritted her teeth and marched on.

Deciding to give the residents of the square a break, she turned down a side street. In a few minutes, Brian's wails turned into quiet sobs, even sadder than the screams. She stopped the stroller, crouched in front of him and said, "There's nothing to be afraid of. It was just a loud sound. It won't happen again. Want to go back and see Dad?"

She turned back toward the diner and heard a wail building up from the stroller. "I guess not," she said, making a swift U-turn. "Then let's go to my house," she said. "How about that?"

"This is above and beyond the call of duty, Allie," Mike said when she called him. "I feel guilty."

"Don't," Allie said. "If he stays at the restaurant, he'll close the place down, and then I won't have a job."

"That's the truth." Mike sighed. "Okay, thanks from the bottom of my heart, and I'll pick him up as early as I can this evening." As an afterthought, he said, "He doesn't have anything to eat."

"The grocery store is a two-block stroller ride from the house. We'll go as soon as it opens. Everything will be fine—"

"What was that?" Mike said, sounding panicked by the deafening sound coming from her kitchen.

Allie put her hand over her other ear. "One pan being banged against another one," she said. "I hope you see the irony here. It's the same kind of sound that scared him this morning."

"Except that this time, *he's* making it. All the difference in the world."

"Just get to work, Mike, and try to relax. I'll call if we need you."

"Okay, Brian," she said enthusiastically when she'd hung up, "give these spoons a try."

Soon after seven she walked him to the store, supplied herself with everything he might need during the course of the day, and congratulated herself that the crisis had passed. He was back to being his old sweet self, fascinated by every "toy" she pulled out of Mrs. Langston's closets and cupboards, which she carefully washed before handing them to him.

When Mike's car pulled up in front of her house at eight that evening, she was lying on the floor beside Brian, gazing at him and thinking hard while he slept in a pile of Mrs. Langston's comforters topped by a clean sheet. She got up to let Mike in and pointed to Brian.

"You know what I'm doing here, don't you?" she asked Mike without even saying hello.

"Saving my life," he guessed.

"No, I'm being the nanny," Allie said. She sighed. "So let's give up, stop pretending I'm not. Between now and January, I'll help you find someone permanent, but for now, I'm it."

She expertly scooped up Brian and laid him across Mike's arms, looking up into his astonished face.

"I'll see you at six tomorrow morning," she said. "Don't argue with me. I'm flat-out exhausted."

She got him onto the stoop and closed the door in his face. And then, unable to help herself, she smiled.

MIKE WAS all ready to go and obviously waiting for her when she arrived at his apartment ten minutes early. He looked cheerful enough holding Brian on his left hip, and Brian waved wildly at her and giggled.

"All quiet on the northern front," Mike murmured.

She took Brian from him, snuggling him and blowing little kisses into his hair. He was clean and sweet-smelling, ready for another fascinating day.

"Did you rest up last night?" he asked her.

"I sat down on my bed to take off my shoes and

fell asleep in my clothes," she admitted. "I feel great now."

And she did feel great. The sight of Mike and Brian together would make anyone feel great.

"There's coffee in the kitchen," Mike said.

Allie glanced up to see Mike gazing at her, his expression unfathomable. "Excellent news," she said.

He smiled at her. "Okay, I'll get down to the kitchen if you think you'll be okay."

"We'll be okay, won't we, Brian?" The baby giggled at her.

"Before you go," she said to Mike, "since I'm officially the nanny now, is there anything you're especially interested in teaching him? Or anything you'd like me to do for him that I might not think of?"

"Well…" He hesitated. "I've been reading The Book, and it says babies should have *activities*. Little League? Piano lessons? I don't think so. Do you know what it's talking about?"

She almost laughed. Instead, she said seriously, "I've heard some of the moms around here talk about swimming lessons in special indoor pools and baby gymnastics classes, and even some learning programs. I'll do some asking around to find out where they're located."

"Thanks. Okay, then, I'll go down to the diner—"

"Then there are play dates with other children, and of course we'll make daily trips out in the stroller now that he's feeling better."

She was suddenly aware that Mike really wanted to go to work. That would change, she was sure. In no time at all, he'd prefer being with Brian to being in the kitchen. She smiled up at him from the floor, where she was already showing Brian how to play with a stacking toy. "Go on," she said. "I know you can't wait to hit the kitchen."

At the top of the stairs, watching him leave, she frowned. He should have kissed Brian goodbye, told him exactly where he was going and when he'd be back. Someday when she felt comfortable about it, she'd mention it to him.

AFTER LUNCH, she put Brian down for a nap and began to straighten up the room, which looked as if poltergeists had attacked it. When the phone rang, she picked it up, then saw her mother's name on the caller-ID screen. Her heart sank. She hadn't confessed to her about her new job. Now she'd been outed.

"Hi, Mom," she said cheerfully, crossing her fingers.

"Allie, I called the diner and they said you were upstairs. What are you doing in Mike's apartment?"

Elaine's voice was calm and pleasant, but Allie could sense that she was nonplussed. "I'm helping Mike with Brian," she hedged. "He's been sick, and he was totally disrupting the cooking and serving, so I offered to stay here with him."

"You've always been good with babies," Elaine said, but her voice was guarded. "But you'll have to be there with him all day, won't you? And well into the night?"

Duh. "Yes, but he's what you call an easy baby," Allie said. "It's not a problem."

"Except that, well, if you end up taking care of him every day so Mike won't have to deal with him in the kitchen, that's a full-time job."

Uh-oh. She had to tell her mother the truth. "I imagine that's the way it'll turn out, Mom. I'll take care of

Brian instead of waiting tables. But during his naptimes I'll be doing my research, and planning the details of the benefit…"

"When you leave in January won't that be upsetting to Brian?"

She couldn't bear to talk about it anymore. Her mother was saying aloud all the worries she'd kept to herself. And the biggest one was Brian would get attached to her—and she was afraid she was already attached to him. Their separation in January could be devastating.

Separating from Mike could be devastating, too.

"Let's cross that bridge when we come to it," she said easily, controlling a tremor in her voice that would give her away.

She heard the sigh at the other end of the line. "The reason I called," Elaine said, "was to ask if I could help you get Mrs. Langston's house cleaned up enough for you to be comfortable there. Priscilla told someone it was filthy when you moved in."

"You're so sweet to offer," Allie said, and she *was* touched by it, "but I won't let you do that. I'm doing a little at a time, and I won't have to clean the whole place, just the rooms I'm using. You just take it easy and raise money for the foster-care center, okay?"

"Come for lunch or dinner sometime, honey. You can bring Brian. What about lunch tomorrow?"

"Thanks, Mom." Allie was surprised. "We'd love to. I'll walk him over in his stroller. About noon?"

"Sounds fine. I'll see you then."

"Mom?" she said hesitantly. "Has anyone in town mentioned how much Brian looks like Mike? I mean, are they, um—"

"Gossiping? Wondering if he is Mike's child in spite

of what he told them about looking like his friend? Oh, yes."

"What about you, Mom? Do you think he is?" She held her breath.

"Well, Allie, do the math," Elaine said rather impatiently. "Brian's eight months old. Eight plus a nine-month pregnancy equals seventeen months. If the mother lived in the valley, *everybody* would know about it. And when has Mike been out of the valley in the last seventeen months? What do you think he's doing, selling sperm to keep the restaurant going?"

"Oh, Mom," Allie said, feeling like laughing and crying at the same time. "Do a little gossiping yourself, and tell the network just what you told me."

"I already have. I laid down the law to that awful Mildred Witherington, so I'm sure everybody's gotten the message by now. Dimwits," she muttered. "They should have realized for themselves how silly the idea was."

Allie hung up, feeling thoughtful. Her mother was a wonderful person, tolerant, forthright and always ready to defend someone she believed in. "I am one lucky woman," she said aloud to the empty room.

MIKE HAD always been able to seem calm on the outside. Now he was constantly twitching and jumping at loud noises. And at six o'clock that evening, he felt that every nerve end was a violin string twanging inside him.

"So what *is* your problem?" he asked himself. For the first time ever, he wanted his workday to be over, wanted to go upstairs and relax as much as he *could* relax with a baby in the house.

Maybe he could. He'd spent most of the day coaching the new interns, who weren't half bad, so the food was cooked. Maury was hard at work, Becky and Colleen were there. He'd give it a try.

"Maury, think you could do without me this evening?"

Maury actually looked pleased. "Sure. You need a break. I'll call you if anything falls apart."

"Maury" came a musical voice from the doorway, "where are the... Oh," she said. "Hi, Mike."

"Hi, Carrie." Becky's daughter had changed in the last few years, too, just as Allie had, and one look at Maury's face said that he'd noticed the changes. No wonder he'd been perfectly happy to have Mike out of the way tonight. He was thinking about stolen moments, warm glances, the touch of hands as plates were handed back and forth. Ah, young love.

Mike started up the stairs, quickly at first, then one leaden step at a time. Was he any different from Maury? Wasn't he imagining stolen moments, warm glances, the touch of hands as he and Allie passed Brian back and forth—

He stopped, leaning against the railing, suddenly tired. Tired of being a restaurateur, tired of being a man with feelings he was afraid to express, most of all, he was tired of being a substitute father.

He hadn't even lasted a week. It wasn't Brian he wanted to be with this evening. It was Allie.

He had to stop it. The point in spending the evening at home was to give Allie a break. And to bond with Brian. He'd send her home at once.

From behind the door he heard Brian shriek, "Urrr."

"Urrr to you, too," Mike said from the doorway.

Allie jumped. She must have caught the twitchiness

from him. He examined the chaos of the room and said, "Are you having a party?" he asked. "Am I invited?"

"Absolutely," Allie said. "Join us, won't you, if you can find space."

Mike felt pretty happy sitting on the floor with Allie and Brian and almost every toy Brian owned. He'd send her home in just a minute. She turned a glowing gaze on him. "Look what he's learned to do. He knows how to pull his train toward him! Good job," she congratulated Brian, and gave him a hug.

"Wow," he said. "Hey, big guy."

"Urr," Brian burbled.

Allie laughed. "I think Brian's going to be an early talker. He's so smart."

Mike stood up. "So am I. I decided to take the evening off."

"Good for you. You can play with Brian while I straighten up."

"Nope. You, young lady, may go home early. The mess will still be here in the morning."

His heart wasn't in it when he said it, and he might have been mistaken, but he thought she looked, well, disappointed.

Except that she recovered so quickly. "I'll have an evening to work on the house. That's awfully nice of you. Are you sure you'll be okay?"

"Absolutely," he lied. "I have The Book."

She smiled. "Promise to call me if anything goes wrong?"

"Nothing will go wrong," he said, doubting it strongly. "Trust me."

She picked Brian up and snuggled him, gave him kisses that made him giggle, then handed him to Mike. Their hands brushed, just as Mike had been hoping they would. She looked up into his face. "I do," she said. "I do trust you." She held his gaze for a second or two, then said, "See you in the morning, Brian." She gave him a final kiss and said to Mike, "He hasn't had dinner yet. And remember you have to share the train."

Once she was gone, Mike admitted to himself how sorry he'd been to see her leave.

"Okay, Brian, what's for dinner?" He carried him into the kitchen and examined the jars of baby food. "How about," he said, showing Brian a jar of puréed chicken, "chicken Marsala, with," and he hefted another jar, "scalloped potatoes, and, let's see what we have here, spinach purée."

Brian babbled at him and reached for the jar of spinach, which gave Mike an idea. "I wonder if you really need to eat this stuff," he said. "I'm going to consult The Book."

With the baby book open on the kitchen counter, he got to the section on foods for babies at various points in their development. "Here we are. Eight months—'At eight months, your baby may have vegetables and fruits you've mashed with a fork.' See," he said to Brian, "if we had some scalloped potatoes up here I could mash them for you.

"'The food shouldn't have any lumps, pieces of skin, strings or seeds.' Hmm. Guess that rules out green beans. Uh-oh, Brian, we're doomed. 'Don't season your baby's food with…' With anything, it sounds like. And it says absolutely no leftovers because they might have bacteria. Guess we'll just have to make do."

He thought he might be getting the hang of this fathering thing. Dinner was a big success, and he managed a bath without drowning the baby.

And at the end of it, he was exhausted. He thought it

might be the constant talking that did it. "A rest period, that's what we need," he told Brian, and yawned. He put the baby, clean and sweet-smelling, into one of the things with feet that crib-dwellers apparently slept in and lifted him into his playpen so Brian wouldn't feel that the fun had ended forever. He added several soft toys, a fuzzy ball—what marketing expert had dreamed up that vile orange color?—a stuffed lamb Ian had brought over and a weird-looking thing Allie had told him was an "educational" toy. Brian seemed happy to be talking to the educational toy.

Mike dropped into the brown leather wing chair, leaned back and put his feet up on the ottoman. He'd just rest a minute, one single minute, and then he'd be up and at 'em again.

Maybe two minutes.

Chapter Eight

He must have fallen asleep, because he was certainly jolted awake by pounding on the front door that was loud enough to be heard two mountain ranges away. Mike's heart slammed against his breastbone as he leapt up and looked into the playpen.

Brian must have been sleeping, too, because he was sitting up now and on the verge of tears, obviously scared by the noise.

Mike rubbed his face, willing his pulse to return to normal, then picked up Brian and settled his chin on the baby's silky red hair. "It's okay," he assured Brian.

He threw open the door and glared at his brothers. Ian, he could tell, was the culprit, because Daniel was standing back, glaring at Ian, too. "Why don't you just kick it in the next time?" Mike said. "Brian was asleep. You scared him."

Ian shrugged. "We got tired of the usual kind of knocking. Dads tend to doze in front of the TV. You have to knock hard to wake 'em up."

Mike's hackles rose. "I wasn't asleep."

"Yes, you were," Ian said. "I could hear you snoring."

"Must have been Brian," Mike muttered. Ian was only

pushing his buttons, and, in fact, he *had* been dozing. Lightly. Not in front of the TV, but close enough.

"Sorry about that," Daniel said, taking Brian and giving him a smacky kiss on each cheek. No longer afraid, Brian giggled, delighted. "Uncle Ian is a real pain, kid. The sooner you learn it, the better."

"Very funny." Ian flopped on the sofa. "So how's it going?"

Mike frowned. "You turned social worker all of a sudden?"

Daniel shoved Ian over and sat next to him, settling Brian in his lap. "We just wanted to see how you are."

Suspicion snaked up Mike's spine. "Why?"

"Because we care about you," Daniel said. "A lot has happened to you lately."

"Yeah, and we're here to make sure you don't have a breakdown." Ian shifted his weight and pulled a stuffed rabbit out from under him. He glared at the rabbit, then at Mike. "Man, this would really get to me. Hey," he protested as Brian lurched for the rabbit and snuggled back onto Daniel's lap, holding it tightly.

It was the rabbit Allie had chosen at the toy store. It was soft and squishy. And washable, she'd told him. The eyes were embroidered on so there were no loose buttons for Brian to swallow. Allie called it Brian's Bunny Buddy. On one of his quick visits upstairs today, he'd found her doing the bunny hop with Brian and the rabbit bouncing up and down in her arms.

He realized he'd been obsessing on the rabbit, or on Allie, when Ian said, "You *have* lost it. I knew it."

Mike pulled his attention away from the rabbit and stared at his brother. He must have had a sentimental expression on his face, because Ian was looking at him as if he'd sprouted wings.

"I haven't lost it," he said crossly, even though he wasn't one-hundred-percent certain about that. When Ian gave him a skeptical look, he added, "Sure, right now I feel like I'm being pulled in a dozen different directions."

Daniel nodded. "Kids will do that. But they're worth the sacrifice. They deserve the best you've got."

Mike nodded. Yeah, he knew that. He'd grown up with the other option, the father who didn't give him anything of himself, much less his best.

He'd do better by Brian, but the pressure on him was immense. It wasn't as if he'd planned to be a father, wanted to be a father. He'd been forced into being one.

Right now he thought he was doing great. But he kept thinking of Brian as someone else's child—which he was—a child Mike was babysitting—which he wasn't—until those people came to pick him up, which would be never.

"I'm trying," he said to Daniel. "Like you said, it's not easy."

"Nothing important ever is." Ian's look was hard, resolute. "Can't screw up this one, Mike."

"I can't screw up anything," Mike retorted. As if he needed more pressure. "But a couple of weeks ago it was just the diner I couldn't screw up, and now it's the diner and the franchise opportunity that won't wait forever and Brian, who needs my full attention."

"Put Brian at the top of that list," Daniel said. "You need to spend more time with him."

"Well, look, here I am," Mike said. "I took the evening off, sent Allie home, we've been playing." He sighed and leaned back in his chair. "But I can't do it every night. Maybe when Barney comes back I can figure out something."

"Can't recapture lost days," Ian said. "Make time now."

Make time now. Talk about easy to say and hard to do.

"Yeah, I know you're right. But how? I'm already exhausted, Maury goes back to school Monday and has football practice until six or so—"

"When do your interns from the culinary school start?"

"They started today, and they're pretty good, but I can't just turn them loose in the kitchen. They're here to learn, not to take over. I have to be available, like, right on top of them."

"Think of someplace you could take Brian this weekend. Away from the diner, so your mind will be on him."

Brian was still clutching the rabbit. Mike wished he had a rabbit to clutch. But Brian didn't seem to mind at all being handed over from Uncle Daniel, who had a billion brain cells of stored information about children, to Mike, who had a billion brain cells of stored information about food, and six, maybe, about children. In fact, Brian smiled up at Mike and cuddled into his arms as if he'd been doing it forever.

Daniel had asked him a question. Or delivered an order, depending on how you looked at it. "Take Brian someplace? Where?"

"Somewhere interesting," Daniel said.

"What's interesting when you're eight months old?"

"Everything," Daniel said.

Ian shrugged. "Someplace that interests you. If you're happy, the kid will be, too."

Daniel gave him a wondering look. Mike suspected that Daniel was surprised that Ian was even taking an interest.

"That would be the kitchen, Ian," Mike said, "which isn't what you're talking about. But actually, The Book—"

"The Book," Ian said.

"Yes." If Ian even tried to make fun of The Book he'd toss him out the window—one of the street-level windows of the diner, of course, which would leave Ian dusty but not maimed. "The Book mentioned activities, and I asked Allie to do some research. She'll find something."

He didn't miss the look Ian and Daniel exchanged, but he could ignore it. Yes, he was responsible for Brian, but he'd hired Allie, who was a responsible person.

Then old memories came back to him, and he thought, *like my parents put me in the care of a responsible person.*

But Allie was different from any nanny *he'd* ever had. He could depend on her. She seemed to know what to do, and what she did always seemed to be okay with Brian.

Something that had been niggling at him suddenly turned into a full-blown worry. Allie was right for Brian, but was Brian right for Allie? How would being Brian's nanny help her sort out her future, help her prepare for a new career?

It was too late and he was too tired to address the question.

"Okay, you guys, now that you've organized my weekend, shove off and let me get this kid to bed."

When, at long last they were gone, Mike tucked Brian into bed, telling him, "I'm a very responsible babysitter. Have you ever had a wet diaper longer than thirty seconds? Don't I feed you well, given what I have to work with? Isn't Allie the best nanny in the world?"

Brian smiled, and his eyelids drooped.

"In the short run," Mike said sadly, "I'm the kind of guy anybody would be willing to leave a kid with, but, little brother, we're in it for the long haul."

ALLIE WAS PLEASED with what she'd accomplished even while missing Brian like crazy and wishing she were with him. And Mike.

She'd scoured the bathroom and gotten the kitchen cleaned up enough to stand walking into it, put the clutter of paper and magazines in the living room into a box and vacuumed her favorite chair.

While she worked, she planned a color scheme for the benefit dinner. All white would have been more formal, but the foliage would be sporting its brilliant fall colors at the time of the benefit, and she'd decided to take advantage of it. The rental company offered rust-colored tablecloths she'd combine with napkins in a soft maple-leaf red-orange and an aspen yellow. She'd alternate the colors at each table. Cream plates, cups and saucers. Centerpieces of chrysanthemums in coordinating colors.

She'd been thinking of Mike and his "gourmet meat and potatoes" menu while she made her choices. The colors would complement the food, as if his cooking even needed complementing. She should check it out with Lilah, though.

She glanced at Mrs. Langston's wall clock, a beautiful

walnut antique. Nine-thirty. She shouldn't call Lilah at this hour. She'd do it in the—

Her cell phone rang. "Lilah!" she said. "I was just wondering if it was too late to call you."

"Almost, but not quite," Lilah said. "Daniel and Ian dropped in on Mike and found him playing daddy tonight, so I thought I'd give you a call and see how you and Brian are getting along."

"He's a lot more fun than a stack of dirty plates," Allie said. "So far, so good. He's the most darling child I've ever known. Happy—well, almost always—curious, smart, cooperative…he's remarkable."

"I'm so glad you're taking care of him," Lilah said. "It's a match made in heaven."

Allie laughed. "Well, I'm certainly enjoying myself. Incidentally—" And she launched into a description of the color scheme she'd just decided to go with.

"Sounds gorgeous," Lilah said. "Warm, cozy colors for a cold fall night. Go with it."

"Thanks. Oh, I have a question for you. Do you have any suggestions for things to do with babies?"

"How odd," Lilah said. "Mike was talking about the same thing."

"It was Mike's own idea. He asked me to look for possibilities. I know about the big attractions all over the state, but I'm wondering if he should start with something low-key and close to home."

"I'll do some thinking," Lilah said. "Daniel and Ian are bugging Mike to take Brian somewhere this weekend."

"I'm sure he'll think of something wonderful," Allie said.

"I just hope it's not a kitchenware store." Lilah

snickered. "Before I hang up, are you happy in Mrs. Langston's house?"

"Oh, yes." Allie sighed. "Bless her heart, she must have kept everything she's ever owned. Maybe everything three generations of collectors have owned. I'm standing here looking at two china cupboards and one of those lighted display cases chock-full of doodads, from china figurines and cut-glass vases to an ashtray that says, 'Welcome to the Grand Canyon.' Plus stuff in the kitchen cupboards and on top of every table—"

"I wonder if Priscilla would like to have a yard sale," Lilah said thoughtfully, "and donate the proceeds to the center." She laughed. "I'm not shy, am I?"

"If I organized it, it would be something nice I could do for her," Allie said slowly.

"If it's for the center, I'll rally the troops. The whole family plus the center volunteers will help you and Priscilla price things. We can do it in no time flat."

"Okay. I'll ask her," Allie said.

"I have a better idea. Your mother's our chief fundraiser, and very, very persuasive."

"As if I didn't know," Allie muttered.

"I'll ask her to approach Priscilla."

When the call ended, Allie sank into her chair, noticing proudly that the cloud of dust was much less dense as the result of her vacuuming. She was tired, but also sort of excited about her life. She'd read in bed last night, a book describing types of jobs in the psychology field, their educational requirements and their limitations. While Brian napped tomorrow, she'd read more of it.

Or, instead, would she find herself washing Brian's clothes, straightening up his toys and making a grocery list of baby foods and supplies? Being the perfect nanny, the way she'd tried to be perfect at any job? She was getting too deeply into the nanny role. She had to focus on finding the perfect career.

"HI, MOM. Meet Brian," Allie said when she and Brian arrived for lunch the next day.

Somehow, Allie wasn't surprised to see her mother's eyes soften. "Well, hello," Elaine said to Brian. "Come right in. I have a present for you." She practically snatched Brian out of his stroller.

Allie left it in the front hall, dumped her coat on top of it and joined them in the living room. Her mother was on the floor with Brian, who had his plump little arms wrapped around the biggest stuffed bear Allie had ever seen. He rolled over with it, then rolled over again, shrieking with joy.

"I think it's a hit," Allie said. "What shall we name it? Bearly There? Bearable?"

When her mother frowned, Allie stooped down to give her a hug. "Hello to you, too," she said. "Thanks, Mom. He loves that bear, and I love you. Thank you again for doing the math. A detective couldn't have done better."

"Mike's a good man. Somebody needs to look out for him." Then her gaze whipped away from Allie and right back to Brian. "Papa Bear," she cooed. "That's what we'll call him, won't we, Brian." She looked at Allie again, her eyes narrowed. "We'll keep him right here at Aunt Elaine's house for you to play with when you visit."

Her message was clear. Allie had a substitute nanny on call and eager for the work. An hour later, she was finally forced to say, "Um, Mom, I think everyone's getting hungry."

"Oh!" Elaine said, leaping up. "I forgot all about lunch."

Allie smiled. Her mother and Brian seemed to be getting along quite well.

MIKE WAS under even more pressure than before. And pressure to do what? Take his kid brother out somewhere next weekend. Just thinking about it exhausted him, packing the diaper bag, putting Brian in the car seat, folding the stroller into the trunk. His left hip, he thought, was permanently skewed in that direction, and Brian would have to get used to other forms of transportation.

"Lilah says you and Brian have a date this weekend," Allie said when she arrived the next morning.

"Right," Mike said. "Dinner and dancing." He threw out his hands in supplication. "I don't know where to take him," he admitted. "Lilah said something about a farm where he could pet the animals, but I don't feel secure about it. What if one of them bites him. You laugh," he said, looking at Allie's face, "but I might bite him the next time he grabs onto my ears and won't let go."

Suddenly she snapped her fingers. "You know, I have an idea. Ever been to Mayhew's Farmer's Market?"

He wrinkled his forehead. "I know about it, of course. But I buy from local folks, so I've never been there. It's over the ridge, right?"

"Yes, near Grafton. It's a wonderful place. They have fruits and vegetables, their own honey and maple syrup and they sell local crafts."

How could she sound so bubbly this early in the morning?

"The Mayhews grow everything themselves. The

farm stand's right in the middle of the fields and the apple orchard, so you can do your own picking if you want to. And," she said, practically licking her lips at the prospect, "it's pumpkin season."

Mike had a brilliant idea of his own. "Go with us, then," he said craftily. "I'll never find it without you."

She hesitated. "I think you need time alone with Brian."

He gave her an aggrieved look. "He and I will be alone and lost, maybe never find our way home again. Think how bad you'll feel."

"I feel," she said, "as if I'm being conned."

"Did it work?"

She smiled. "Yep. Like magic. Okay, let's do it. Saturday between two and five?"

"Thanks for asking," he said, rubbing it in and feeling pretty good about his people skills. "I'd like that a lot."

Allie narrowed her eyes. "I think I've figured out why the diner is such a success. It's not the food, it's you."

ALLIE CLIMBED out of Mike's station wagon and filled her lungs with the sweet, apple-scented fall air. Mayhew's Farmer's Market was exactly as she remembered it. The exterior was beaten and weathered from surviving so many tough Vermont winters, but inside, the lights shone brightly on towers of gleaming apples, fat squashes, all kinds of potatoes and mouthwatering mounds of heritage tomatoes.

The place was packed, inside and out. Behind the old store stood the greenhouses that kept Mayhew's supplied with lettuces, spinach, green beans and other vegetables when they were out of season.

Behind the greenhouses were the apple orchards, and beside them, her favorite place, the pumpkin patch.

She glanced over her shoulder at Mike, who seemed to be getting out of the car pretty fast himself. One look at him and she knew he was hooked. His eyes had glazed over. Food. Fresh, good food. How could he not be interested?

"Don't forget Brian," she said pointedly.

"Oh, right, Brian," he said, and hurriedly pulled out the stroller and settled the boy into the seat. "Okay, buddy," he said enthusiastically. "Let's go get us a pumpkin."

The day was slightly overcast with a slight chill in the air, a perfect day for exploring the market. They went first to the tables in front, which groaned under the burden of brightly colored vegetables.

Brian was delighted. His hands reached for everything Allie held out for his inspection. She was glad she'd come with them, because Mike was transfixed by the display. "Those fingerling potatoes look good. I'll get some for dinner. Boil them, then at the last minute, frizzle them in olive oil." He picked up six baskets and dumped them into a paper bag.

"Don't touch the purple potatoes." The words came from a tall, rugged man with short white hair. Meriwether Mayhew had been a naval officer, and when he retired, he did an unlikely thing—started an organic farm, which he ran with the same authority he'd had as a military man. His wife, his sons and daughters and their kids all helped out, but "Mer" Mayhew was still the man in charge.

With a look of disgust, he began throwing the offending purple potatoes into a trash can. "Those potatoes are past their prime," he said. "My daughter's kids don't know a potato from a Pokemon." He sighed. "Guess they can't all grow up to be farmers."

He turned to look at Allie. "Well," he said, the twinkle returning to his light-blue eyes. "I know this face." He turned to Mike. "Allie's been coming here since she was so young she kept tumbling over the pumpkins and falling into the vines." He studied Mike for a moment. "You're Mike Foster, right? I've been to your diner a few times. Tasty food, ay-uh, it is."

Mer hunkered down so that he was at eye-level with Brian. "But this young man's new to me." He gave Allie a quizzical look. "Is he—"

"He's Mike's ward," Allie said smoothly, "and I'm temporarily taking care of him."

"I wouldn't have guessed it," Mer said, looking up at Mike. "He's the spitting image of you."

Mike's smile faded. Allie's heart sank, realizing he was quite aware of the resemblance—how could he not be—and perhaps also aware of the gossip. In spite of her mother's certainty that Mike could not have fathered Brian, she would have to ask him pointblank, even if it made him mad enough to put her out of his life.

"I want Brian to see the pumpkin patch," she said quickly. "You know how I always loved it."

Mer solemnly shook Brian's hand. "Pleased to meet you, sir. You folks have a good time, and you find anything as over-the-hill as those potatoes were, you bring 'em to me."

"Interesting man," Mike said. "He cares about quality."

"So do you," Allie said.

"This is a tomato, Brian," Mike said, holding out a creased, lumpy heirloom variety for Brian's inspection. "It's the best kind, not pretty but it tastes better than—"

With one enthusiastic swing of his hand, Brian knocked the tomato to the rough plank floor.

Allie gasped and dived for it, holding it carefully as if it were an injured bird. It had split neatly at the base and fanned out over her hand, dripping juice and seeds. Mike gazed at it for a second or two, while the aroma of lushly ripe tomato filled the air. "Okay, we'll buy that one," he said to Brian. "Excellent choice."

Allie dumped the tomato into a bag and dashed to the counter for paper towels. She'd pay for it first, then clean up the mess and toss it in the trash. When she got back, Mike was gently putting a large basket of the tomatoes into a bag. She began wiping tomato juice off the floor and looked up to see his eyes on her.

"You knew you could sucker me in, didn't you?" His chin dimpled when he smiled. "I get carried away about food."

"Really? I hadn't noticed."

"Okay, I deserve that. You know, I'd like to talk to Mayhew about supplying the diner. Do you mind if I..."

"Not at all." She took the handles of the stroller from Mike. "You'll probably find Mer in the office. Brian and I will do some craft shopping while you're busy."

She grabbed a paper bag from a stack nearby, and staying to the center of the aisle to keep Brian's busy hands away from the merchandise, she selected a box of maple butternut fudge for her mother. Then she gravitated toward the display of handmade candles.

She picked up an evergreen-scented candle. Brian sniffed deeply, smiled, babbled and managed to get his hands around it. "Christmas," she murmured to him. "You're smelling Christmas."

He was almost nine months old now. He'd been born to Mike's friend and his wife at a time when a Christmas tree might still have been up in their house. A bell chimed in her head. Mike's friend must have had a wife, because they'd had a baby.

She might have died in the accident, too. That is, if Mike actually had a friend who'd bequeathed Brian to him. He'd offered no details whatsoever about the funeral or any other aspect of his trip to Boston.

In spite of her mother's defense of Mike, her worry increased.

"We'll take this Christmas candle home," she said, and popped it into the shopping bag.

Mike moved up behind her. She didn't have to look. She could feel him there. She turned to see his face glowing with satisfaction. "You cut a deal with Mer?" she said.

He nodded and took back the handles of Brian's stroller. "I'll buy vegetables in season from the valley locals and he'll take care of the rest. I was about to buy a couple of bushels of apples when he told me that Mildred's been buying her apples from him all along. He strongly suggested that I not tell her I know she's a traitor. We have perfectly good apples in the valley."

"How right he is," Allie said, having dealt with Mildred a couple of times in Mike's absence.

"Mer said to leave our stuff on the counter and go for the pumpkin patch," he said.

"Ummu dok uhnnl," Brian said, which Allie interpreted as "and about time."

The rows of pumpkins were as neat as pumpkin rows

can be. The vines trailed everywhere, patches of green among the orange of the pumpkins.

"What do you think, Brian?" she said, letting Mike push the stroller down the wide dirt paths. "Aren't they pretty?"

Brian burbled his approval.

She turned to Mike. "I remember looking for the perfect pumpkin, but the truth is that pumpkins aren't perfect," she said. "One day my parents got so impatient—they had other things to do—that my mom was about to lose it when Mer came out and explained that pumpkins have their own quirks that make them special."

"Like people," Mike said.

Something in his voice made her nervous. "This one, for example," she rushed on. The pumpkin in question was bumpy and squashed. "She's shorter, but wishes she were taller. She's self-conscious, which you can tell by the way she's let the vines grow over her."

"You think maybe she looks at the vines as her protectors from rejection?"

The way he gazed at her made her nervous and happy at the same time. Allie cleared her suddenly tight throat and said, "She's not afraid of rejection. She's made up for what she lacks in height by being a wonderfully deep orange color." She pulled the pumpkin off the vine. "I'm choosing this one." Remembering their reason for being here, she added, "Brian, which pumpkin looks like you?"

She paused and gazed at Mike, and she knew she'd found the right moment to put her doubts to rest. "Mike," she said slowly, "you're not Brian's father, are you?"

His eyes widened, but he didn't flinch. "When would I have had time to father a child? And with whom? And if I had, I sure wouldn't have forgotten to pick him up for eight months."

She was so relieved she almost laughed. "That's what my mother said," she told him.

"Did you actually think I'm the kind of man who'd refuse to marry the mother of my child?" Now his expression was serious.

"No. I knew you weren't. I believe in you, Mike, and trust you. If you were a pumpkin," and she softened her voice, "you'd be everyone's first choice."

He took a step closer to her until they were almost touching. She didn't know who made the first move, but suddenly his lips were against hers, his arms wrapping around her and pulling her close.

A jolt of surprise danced through her, but she ignored it. So what if kissing Mike wasn't smart? Who said she had to be smart all the time? She'd wanted this kiss for what seemed like forever.

As the kiss deepened, she slid her arms around his neck, feeling his body pressing closer to hers. She sensed he was giving her everything he felt in his heart at that magical moment. She knew she was. "I shouldn't be doing this," he breathed into her ear, "but I don't care."

His mouth joined with hers again, giving her no time to analyze what he'd said, leaving her breathless and hopeful.

"Yah," Brian said gleefully, returning her to real life.

It returned Mike to real life, too. His voice was shaky when he broke off the kiss and took a step back, his eyes still fixed on her face. "Allie, what just happened, I think—"

She sensed what was coming, so she rushed to stop

him. "We shouldn't make a big deal out of it. It was a kiss, a lovely kiss on a beautiful afternoon. Let's just leave it at that."

For a heartbeat, she thought he was going to argue with her, but his face smoothed out, and he nodded. With a slight smile, he gestured toward Brian, who was kicking his heels against the stroller and staring at a gigantic, lopsided, not-quite-ripe pumpkin.

"So that's the one, is it?" Allie asked. Her voice was unsteady.

"Why do you think he likes that one?" Mike sounded shaken, too.

"It's big and silly-looking. You can't help feeling happy when you look at it." She couldn't help feeling happy, but the pumpkin wasn't the reason. "Pick one for yourself," she told him, her knees still feeling wobbly, her heart still zinging.

"Okay." He knelt down, then looked back up at her. "And one for Maury."

She was touched that he would think to take a pumpkin home to Maury. He was like a father to the boy. He would learn to be a terrific father for Brian. She was sure of it.

Chapter Nine

The next few weeks flew by in Fast Forward. Allie spent too much time daydreaming about Mike, but she still managed to get a lot done on the benefit. She'd whipped together the last arrangements, thrilled that the space would be filled to capacity. Enthusiastic volunteers had agreed to pick their chrysanthemum plants down to the ground to make centerpieces for the eight tables, and the feed store in Holman was loaning them potted mums to scatter around the room.

She'd learned from Maury that the Churchill Consolidated High School had a string quartet. With trepidation, she'd hired them for the dinner, and even if they were awful, four students had netted her eight parents who bought tickets for the dinner.

The plan was in place, ready to be implemented, until the last-minute crises occurred, which they would, because they always did.

As for the other two things on her mind, Priscilla had been enthusiastic about the yard sale. "Mother was thrilled to be doing something for the foster-care center. She's already furnished her room with her favorite things, and I'll keep the family heirlooms and a few other pieces I'm fond of. The rest can go. Once I get them out of the way, the cleanup will be a lot easier. Can you get along without some of the furniture?"

"If you leave the bed, one of the sofas and that wing chair in the living room, I'll be fine." Allie smiled. "Maybe I can get my mother to buy them when I move out."

Priscilla, Lilah and her "troops" showed up after school on the Thursday afternoon before the sale. Mike was in the forefront of Allie's mind as she helped dust and price items. He'd been all she could think about this week. Her body had tingled each time she heard his name or saw his face.

He was a dedicated man who also happened to be charming, irresistible, actually. He only became more irresistible the day he announced that he'd be taking two afternoons off each week to be with Brian. He was entertaining him this afternoon, in fact, taking him to a baby gymnastics program in Rutland.

Allie lived for the promise of those two afternoons. She cherished the time she spent with Mike and Brian, and knew deep down that her world currently revolved around two things: making Brian happy and spending time with Mike.

It was dangerous territory. Her world might revolve around them now, but in a few months, she'd have to shift her axis, feel the pull of her classwork.

She wanted a husband and children, but not right now. It was impossible, the daydream of becoming part of the Foster family that had plagued her recently.

Maybe she was just confused and lost at the moment, so daydreaming about Mike and Brian gave her something to do besides worry. She couldn't imagine *not* having a career that would make a difference in the world beyond the family she longed to have. She wasn't even sure what career path she wanted to pursue, although she was finding the idea of clinical psychology increasingly appealing.

It would take years of study. She'd have to get a doctorate. She'd have to train under a practicing psychologist. Brian would be in school by the time she finished. He wouldn't remember her by then.

Mike would have to take over from her. He'd hire a new nanny to take care of Brian while he worked, but he'd have to be the important person in Brian's life. He was wonderful to Brian, but something was missing. If Brian *had* been his own child or a planned adoption, he'd feel different. But how could anyone keep from loving Brian? Because that's what was missing—the sense that Mike truly loved the baby.

"I'M GOING CRAZY being at home all the time," Barney grumbled, shifting his recliner to an upright position. "I want to get back to work."

Mike couldn't wait to have Barney in the kitchen again, but only if he was up to it. "Are you sure you should come back that soon?" he asked, for probably the tenth time.

"The doc said part-time starting Monday. You want him to write me a note?" Barney grumbled. "I won't lift anything. I won't stand too long. But being out and moving and doing what I like to do will be great for the old ticker."

Mike could see how that could help. "Okay, if you're sure, and if you promise not to overdo. And no sneaking any fried foods."

Barney nodded glumly. "Yeah, it's all grilled chicken breasts and greens for me from now on."

He looked so crestfallen that Mike chuckled. "Cheer

up. You know I can cook a chicken breast that will make you forget all about steak."

Barney glared at him. "Prove it to me."

"Just watch me. You'll be fine if you change your diet and exercise."

"That's what the doc says. You two been talking behind my back?" A sneaky smile suddenly appeared on his face. "How's Allie?"

The unexpected change of topic surprised Mike. "Fine. She's taking care of Brian for me."

"Bet you're glad she's back in town, aren't you?"

Okay, he might not be the sharpest knife in the drawer, but Mike knew when someone was baiting him. "What are you talking about?"

Barney shrugged. "The whole town's been watching you two fall for each other."

Mike's mouth dropped open. "Whoa! The whole town knows? How could—wait a minute. We haven't fallen for each other. Allie and I are good friends, that's all."

Barney snorted. "Just friends. Got it."

Mike let it go because he knew there was no sense in arguing with Barney. The older man had been through a lot, and fighting with his employer couldn't be good for his heart.

But Barney was wrong. Mike had noticed how attractive…make that beautiful…Allie was. But it wasn't like they were falling for each other. Not at all. Sure, they'd shared a couple of kisses, but the time he'd kissed her after the crisis with Brian didn't count. He'd been so strung-out he didn't know what he was doing.

Now the kiss in the pumpkin patch—but that didn't mean anything. Even Allie had said it didn't mean anything.

He stood, more than ready to leave, when someone knocked on the door. "I'll answer it," Mike said, and to his amazement, Elaine Hendricks stood on the porch.

He was almost too startled to let her in, but he managed. "I just came by to drop off a little something for Barney to eat," she said. She was bent to one side from the weight of a tote bag that Mike could see was stuffed with storage containers, and she was blushing. He turned to glance at Barney. Talk about color in his face. He was scarlet.

"That's mighty nice of you, Elaine," he said.

"It's all very healthy," she said, sounding a little breathless. "I even found a cake recipe that's made with olive oil. I'll just put the bag in the kitchen and be on my way."

"No, no," Mike protested. "I was just leaving. Bye, Barney."

"Look for me in the diner bright and early next week," Barney said. He said it sheepishly, but then he scowled. "And that grill had better be clean."

"I'll scour it myself," Mike promised. "I don't trust anybody else."

Elaine was certainly taking a long time to put a tote bag on the counter. Time for him to leave so she'd stay and visit with Barney.

Elaine and Barney? Should he spread the rumor? Nope. They were probably—just good friends.

DESPITE THE COLD and the early hour, the garden behind Mrs. Langston's house was crawling with people. What furniture they were selling had gone quickly. Now all that was left were piles of smaller household items, tables filled with clothing and linens and a mountain of books.

"Boy, you don't mess around, do you?" Allie turned to Lilah. "Have you ever considered running for President? You really know how to get people to go along with you. This turnout is amazing."

Priscilla had decided not to come to the sale, thinking that seeing her mother's things go might make her sad, so Lilah sat in one of the wooden chairs behind the cashier's table tallying up what they'd made so far. "It isn't hard when what you're doing supports such a good cause. I'm worried though, because business is slowing down now that the furniture is gone."

Allie sat in the chair next to hers. "It's still early," she said. "But frankly, a lot of what's left is junk."

"They are valuable heirlooms," Lilah said, turning a stern face in Allie's direction. "Once-in-a-lifetime purchases."

Allie had to laugh at that. She could see from the disinterested expressions of some of the shoppers that the words *valuable heirlooms* weren't what they were thinking.

"Gee, I'm not sure how we'll convince them," Allie said. She looked around, trying to come up with some ideas, when she spotted Mike and Brian walking toward her. As usual, her heart fluttered at the sight of Mike. He was drop-dead gorgeous, and all she could think about was kissing him again.

"You've got quite a turnout," Mike said when he reached their table.

"Yes, but the buying has slowed down." Allie leaned over and nuzzled Brian's cheek. "How are you guys today?"

She'd taken the day off for the sale, but she had to admit she didn't really want the day off. She'd rather spend it with her two special guys.

"We're good," Mike said. "Had a cereal fiasco this morning, but everything is fine now."

"Brian didn't want to eat his cereal?" Allie asked.

Mike smiled and bounced the baby on his hip. "Let's just say we had different ideas about what should be done with the cereal. My vote was for eating it. Brian thought tossing it around the room was a better approach."

Lilah laughed and held out her arms to take Brian. "What a mischief you are."

"Said like a person who didn't spend an hour scraping cereal off the floor," Mike said dryly.

"I know how we can take your mind off the cereal," Lilah said, shooting a conspiratorial smile toward Allie. "Help us persuade our customers to buy, buy, buy."

Mike looked around. "Persuade them, huh?"

"Yes, apparently Lilah feels what we have for sale here are heirlooms. We just need to help people see their potential," Allie told him.

"Okay, I'll try if you'll try," he said to Allie.

Although she had no idea how to be a super salesperson, she wanted to follow Mike wherever he was going. Standing, she circled the small table. "You go first."

Mike surveyed the crowd, then walked over to a middle-aged couple standing near an assortment of old pails. Since Allie didn't recognize them, they had to be out-of-towners, and she was sure Mike had chosen them for that very reason.

"I want these pails," he said loudly to Allie. "I'll pot plants in them next summer and put them on the back porch."

The couple turned their attention to the pails.

"Rustic chic," Allie trilled. "Very trendy."

He glanced at a price tag. "These are authentic. I'll take them all."

"Excuse me," the woman said, "but we'd already decided to buy the pails."

Mike turned to Allie. "I'll pay you double the price."

"No," Allie said sternly, "that wouldn't be fair. These people saw them first. I'm upset that you'd even suggest such a thing."

The couple gathered up the pails, all nine of them, and darted toward Lilah at the cash register. Nonplussed, Lilah sent a glance toward Mike and Allie.

"That went well," Allie said.

"Just need to help people see the value of a rusty pail." His eyes twinkled. "Your turn," he said. "Let's see you in action," and he stepped toward the cash register, where Daniel had begun helping Lilah pack those pails in newspaper as if they were treasured objects.

Rising to the challenge, Allie spotted a group of potential buyers. She approached the teenaged girls with a smile. "Have you looked through the clothes?"

The girls looked horrified. "They're for *old* people."

"They're vintage," Allie said. "Have you priced vintage clothes at that shop in Woodstock?" She picked up an elegant blue cocktail dress that looked as if it dated back to the fifties. "Imagine yourself wearing this to the Homecoming Dance. One of a kind, no one else will have anything like it."

"I'm buying my dress at the mall in Manchester," one of the girls said, eyeing the blue dress dubiously.

"Me, too," the other one said. They wandered off to look into a box of DVDs.

One girl stayed, her eyes fixed on the dress. "I'd like something different for the dance and I really can't afford anything from the mall. I love this color, but

I'm not sure about—" She tweaked one of its puffed sleeves.

"Picture it without the sleeves," Allie said. She looked at the price tag. "And even though it's an expensive designer dress, it's only five dollars."

The girl still looked uncertain, but Allie spotted a talented local seamstress going through the linens. "Let's ask Marion what you could do with this dress. I bet she could alter it to suit you, and you'd still have paid a lot less than what you'd pay for a cookie-cutter dress at the mall."

The girl nodded with excitement, and in a few minutes, Marian and the girl had decided how to make the blue dress into something stunning for the Homecoming Dance. Allie felt good about what she'd done, and furthermore, every woman at the sale was at the clothing table, going through Mrs. Langston's dresses.

When Allie rejoined Mike, he nudged her lightly. "You're getting the hang of this. Should we take our act on the road?"

"Hey, Allie, want to come over for dinner tonight?" Daniel asked, coming over to join them. "Mike and Brian will be there."

Mike shot his brother a pointed look, then turned to Allie. "Not to babysit," he said. "To eat."

"I'm not sure I'd know how to eat without a baby on my lap," Allie said, smiling at Mike's flushed face. "I wish I could, but—" oh, she hated saying no "—I promised Mom I'd come to dinner after the sale. She wants to crow over the treasures she took home." She felt like teasing Mike because he looked so uptight about the babysitting idea. "Want me to take Brian with me?"

"No," chorused all three brothers and Lilah, who'd stepped up behind them.

Laughing, Allie stepped toward the table of thread-bare linens, and was soon pointing out the hand-cro-cheted trims on the pillowcases. "You could put this on a little girl's dress," she said to potential buyers, "and turn it into something special."

DINNER AT Daniel's house always included a soccer game. Boys were everywhere, running, laughing and playing. In the middle of the commotion was the family dog, barking and running around the backyard.

Today, in addition to Mike and Brian, there were Ian, Daniel, Lilah, the foster boys and a few of their friends, Lilah's son Jonathan, and Jesse, the elderly ex-Marine who helped care for the boys.

No wonder Allie hadn't wanted to come. There wasn't room.

Mike settled on the back stoop and watched the soccer game. Brian sat on his lap, apparently delighted at all the sights and sounds around him.

"He's going to be walking in a few months," Lilah said, sitting next to him. "Maybe sooner. And then after walking comes running."

Mike shuddered. "I have enough trouble keeping up with him when he crawls. I can't even think about running."

Daniel came over and stood by his wife. "Ha, that's nothing. Wait until he learns to drive a car."

That was it. "Now you're just trying to bug me," he told Daniel.

"True." He leaned down and took Brian from Mike. "He seems to be settling in okay."

Mike shrugged. "I guess. I hope so. We seem to be doing fine, but I worry all the time. Like at any second something could go wrong."

"It could," Ian said.

"Ian!" Lilah scolded him. "Just keep an eye on him. Babies and toddlers are curious, but they don't have a smidgen of common sense. And you have no idea how fast they can move when they're motivated."

Mike sighed. "That's what I'm worried about. I tend to get to thinking about food and the restaurant and go off into my own world."

"When you hear a loud crash, you'll come right back into this one," Ian said.

"Ian, you're scaring him," Lilah said.

"He can't scare me," Mike said. "I'm already scared."

Daniel laughed. "Don't worry. Your protective instincts will kick in, and pretty soon you'll be able to think food and Brian at the same time."

"You're doing a great job, Mike," Lilah said. "Let up on yourself."

As if to agree, Brian waved his arms and smiled, two deep dimples forming on his face. The kid was cute, and from what he'd read in The Book, learning at a rate well above the average. Besides, he rarely cried, slept well and ate like a champ.

Maybe that was why Mike couldn't shake the feeling that such a great kid deserved so much more than he had to offer.

"Allie's around to help," Daniel said. "She'll make certain you do what you need to do."

"Remember, Allie won't be here long." It was a reminder to himself as well as to Daniel. "She'll go back to college in January."

"You'll find another nanny by then," Daniel said. "There's nobody like Allie, though, so treasure her while you can."

Treasure Allie. He did. He loved being around her, enjoyed talking with her and respected her opinions. He shouldn't have kissed her, but there she'd been, so close, looking up at him and so beautiful in the sunlight…

It was the *while you can* part that made him reluctant to get any closer to her, physically or emotionally. She'd be gone in January, and he'd still be here. He'd always be here. He was aware of his own vulnerability, the longing for love to replace the love his parents hadn't shown toward him. He loved his brothers, but it wasn't enough. He couldn't let himself get to the point that Allie's leaving would break his heart, make him feel again like the neglected child he'd been.

Mike noticed that Brian was sagging in Daniel's arms, fighting to keep his eyes open. He took the baby from Daniel and put him to bed in the portable crib he always had with him, stashed in the back of the wagon just in case. Brian went right to sleep, so Mike went back outside, leaving the door open so he could hear if Brian started to cry.

"My life used to be so simple," Mike said when he sat back down on the steps. "Downstairs in the morning, upstairs at night…"

"Sounds dull," Ian said.

"Yeah, well, now your life is interesting," Daniel pointed out. "And an interesting life beats a dull one any day."

Mike considered what his brother had said as he watched the soccer game. The boys were running, the dog was barking and general pandemonium reigned. Daniel's life was way too interesting for him.

But maybe a small dose of "interesting" really was a good thing. He and Brian were getting along okay. And Allie…well, Allie added a very special kind of interesting element to his life, one he would always remember.

ALLIE WAS TERRIFIED, and it was her own fault. When she'd gotten home from dinner with her mother, she'd been restless. What she'd really wanted to do was go to Daniel's house and see if she was in time for dessert. But she knew that would be foolish—and more than a little desperate—so she'd settled on the couch and put the only DVD left over from the sale into the player.

Surprisingly and unfortunately, Mrs. Langston was a horror-film buff, so now Allie was huddled in the corner of the couch, an afghan half hiding her face as she watched *The Shining.*

"You're an idiot," she told herself. She didn't have to watch it. All she had to do was turn it off. But here she was, still watching it.

A car pulled up in front of her house. In any other circumstance she wouldn't even have heard it, but now, in her state of terror, she cast her eyes wildly around the room for a suitable weapon, heavy, scary-looking, but non-lethal. When she heard footsteps coming toward the house, she stopped considering options and hoisted a yard-sale reject, Mrs. Langston's flowered metal umbrella stand, over her head.

As she expected—a slow, ominous knocking at the door. Weapon at the ready, she peered through the peephole in the door to see in the porch light that the wicked supernatural creature she was ready to take on was, in fact, Mike, with Brian on his hip and a box in his other hand, which explained why he'd had difficulty knocking.

She was even more thrilled to see him than usual. She opened the door, feeling idiotic. "Hi," she said lamely, ushering them in.

Mike's gaze gravitated to the umbrella stand she still

clutched in her arms. "Rearranging the accessories?" he asked her.

"Oh. No. Things got a bit scattered after the sale. I'm just…umm, what brings you here?"

"Lilah wanted you to have some leftovers from dinner tonight. She insisted I stop by on my way home," Mike said, carrying the box to the kitchen. "Hope you don't mind."

"Mind free food? Cooked by somebody else? Who could mind?" Allie took the plastic storage containers from the box. Inside she found leftover meat loaf, potatoes and green beans.

"Wow, she must really think I need food," Allie said as she placed the dishes in the refrigerator.

"No, it was her none-too-subtle ploy to get me to stop by and check on you," Mike said, not looking unhappy about his fate.

"Oh, really? Now why would she want to do that?"

Mike met her gaze straight-on. "I think she's match-making."

Allie was almost holding her breath when she asked, "How do you feel about that?"

"How do *you* feel about it?"

Truthfully, Allie wasn't sure. "It's sweet that she's interested. I think she just wants everybody to be as happy as she and Daniel are."

Mike just looked at her for a moment, his gaze so intent it felt like a touch. Allie took a step toward him, but Brian, who was sleepy and fussing, flung his arms at her, so instead of her latching on to Mike, Brian latched on to her.

"I think he's hungry," she said when he began chewing on her shirt.

"Hungry for his fourth or fifth meal of the day. Mind if I feed him something before I leave?"

"Not at all. In fact, why don't I put out a snack for us, too." She hesitated. "Want some pie? You could stay for a while. I was watching a movie—" she hesitated again "—sort of. You could watch it, too."

Mike nodded. "Sure. You were 'sort of' watching it? How does somebody—"

"I'll hold him while you get the things from the car," she said hurriedly.

While she distracted Brian, Mike went to the car and brought in the portable crib and a diaper bag. They soon had the baby changed, fed and sitting sleepily in his crib, which they put right beside the couch where they sat side-by-side, eating wedges of apple pie Allie had warmed in the oven while they were taking care of Brian.

"This is a terrific pie. Did you make it?" Mike asked her.

"Are you kidding? Mom sent the leftovers home with me. I did make one once. I could have piled the apples in a box and it would have tasted just as good."

He laughed. "What movie were you 'sort of' watching?"

"*The Shining.* Want me to start it over?"

Mike shook his head. "No, I've seen it several times. Just start where you left off."

While Mike carried their empty plates to the kitchen, Allie, already longing for her afghan shield, resumed playing the movie. Mike settled next to her on the couch, and soon he was engrossed in the film.

Allie was thinking that she couldn't pull up the afghan in front of Mike, and she couldn't suggest an alternative entertainment option, when she noticed that Brian had fallen asleep.

"I don't think he likes the movie," she whispered.

Mike dimmed the table lamp near the crib. "He doesn't know what he's missing."

She hoped he never would. He was missing Jack Nicholson chasing his family, a trauma that would never happen to him. She couldn't stand it anymore. She grabbed the afghan and turned her face to one side, where Mike's shoulder loomed not an inch away.

"I can't watch," she moaned.

"Scaredy cat," Mike said.

"I hate horror movies." She pulled the afghan up tighter.

"Then why are you watching it?"

"It was all I had, and I needed something to distract me."

She looked up and found Mike watching her intently. She could see desire on his face, and felt the same flame of awareness race through her.

"Distract you from what?" he said, and his voice was hoarse.

"Oh, things," she said distractedly, "things like—"

"I should take Brian home now," he said in that same crackly, hesitant voice.

Of course he should. The sensible side of her knew that. But she couldn't hear her sensible voice speaking to her, only the sensual one, and she listened to it, wanting him more than she could bear.

Their eyes met and held, and gazing at him, she knew there was only one right thing to do. "Don't leave," she whispered, leaning up and brushing his lips with hers. "Stay here with me."

Chapter Ten

Allie knew Mike wanted to stay, and knew he shouldn't. She knew she shouldn't have asked him, but she couldn't help herself.

"All we can count on having, Mike, is *now*," she whispered. "Time's going fast. I'll go back to school, and you have earthshaking decisions of your own to make. We don't know what will happen, so we have to make the most of the time we have."

Whether it was because she'd convinced him or because he no longer had the willpower to resist, Allie wasn't sure, but he wordlessly gathered her in his arms and kissed her deeply.

She'd never felt so cherished, so adored, as she did with him. His kisses were slow and leisurely, his intent to please her obvious.

She broke away from him, stood and took his hand. Her gaze still locked on his, she led him to her bedroom. Once there, she turned and kissed him again. She was starving for him, but she wanted to savor this moment, wanted to remember every second of it.

Slowly she helped him with his clothes, and shivered with pleasure as he slid hers away from her. Together on the softness of the sheets, she explored his body, loving the feel of his skin, the taste of his kisses. He kissed her softly, shifting so he could run his hands down her body, caressing every curve, making her breath catch in her throat.

"I've dreamed about this," he said softly. "Since you came back, I've been fighting not to touch you, not to kiss you."

"Don't fight anymore," she said, gasping slightly when he trailed his lips across her right breast.

He made a low moaning sound and captured her taut nipple between his lips. He slid one hand across her abdomen, settling between her legs. His touch was magic, teasing and stroking Allie until she was desperate for release. Slowly he fanned the flames of her desire until she felt ready to explode.

When she couldn't take it any longer, she opened the drawer in her bedside nightstand and took out a condom. He shot her a quizzical look.

"I've been hoping my dreams would eventually turn into reality," she said simply.

Her confession earned her a kiss, and then another. Finally, when she thought she couldn't take the torment any longer, he joined their bodies. Nothing had ever felt so right, so perfect, as being with him. They moved as if they'd been making love for years, their bodies in tune with each other. When she was desperate for breath, he made one last thrust, bringing them both to the release they so desperately craved.

Afterward, they lay quietly, Allie cuddled within the circle of his arms, contentment filling her. Tonight had been wonderful. More than wonderful. Her last thought before she fell asleep was that even if what she had with Mike couldn't last forever, she finally knew what it was like to love someone completely.

THE SOUND of Brian whimpering woke Mike. He opened his eyes, and then wanted to close them again. Allie. He'd slept with Allie. It had been wonderful and amazing, but he also worried it had been a mistake. What if he ended up hurting her?

He would never hurt her. He had to face up to it. What he was worrying about was *her* hurting *him*. Later, when Allie woke up, he'd talk to her about never repeating what happened last night. He'd have to be very clear about that.

He climbed out of bed, got dressed and went to check on Brian. With ease, after so many weeks of practice, he soon had the baby diapered. He carried Brian on his hip as he went back to the bedroom.

Allie was awake and dressed. She smiled at him.

"Good morning," she said brightly.

Mike opened his mouth to tell her that last night was a mistake, but the words wouldn't come. Instead, he crossed the room and kissed her.

So much for making it clear.

"Good morning," Mike said. "Sorry about—"

Allie laughed. "Don't say it." Her voice quieted. "It was a wonderful night. I'll never forget it."

Neither would he. Would he have the strength to stop at one wonderful night? He had a feeling he wouldn't.

"We have to go home," he said.

The brightness faded from her face.

"We don't want to go home, but we have to."

"But…why?"

He moved closer, looked into her eyes and said, "Because, beautiful woman, my car has been parked outside your house all night. If we leave right now, we might get away with it."

Her eyes widened. "I never thought of that. The

telephone brigade could spread the news all over the valley by noon."

"Right. So I'm going home, and—"

"Will you ever come back?"

"I shouldn't, but I wouldn't be surprised if I did." He smiled at her, ran his hand over her hair then cupped her chin with his hand. "In fact, I wouldn't be surprised if I went home, improved on Brian's and my grooming and then came back here to pick you up. For a nice day with Brian's nanny."

Her eyes narrowed. "You sound like a man with experience in this sort of thing."

"Yes," he said, "and this is it. My experience." He tapped his forehead. "I just think fast."

She laughed at him. "Go, then. I'll see you later."

Mike packed Brian's things in the car and went back for the baby. Driving home, he knew he was the happiest he'd ever been, but he still couldn't shake the feeling that he shouldn't have let last night happen.

ALLIE SPENT all day Sunday with Mike and Brian. Maury and the interns ran the diner, and Mike only called three times and stopped in twice to check on them. "Taking a day off with Brian," he'd explained to them early in the morning, "with Allie along for moral support."

They went for a drive in the country to admire the leaves, stopped by a cold, clear stream for a picnic lunch Allie had put together from Lilah's leftovers—meat loaf sandwiches being the main course and her mother's pie for dessert. They listened to the water bubbling over the rocks while they ate, and spent the rest of the afternoon at her house watching Brian pull himself up on the furniture.

"He'll be walking before you know it," she marveled.

"Lilah already warned me," Mike said, and his glum tone of voice made her laugh.

During these innocent pursuits, her body zinged with sexual energy. She wanted more of him, so much more, and soon. Mike cooked dinner—a simple but wonderful pasta dish with white clam sauce, and then they watched a G-rated movie on TV with Brian cuddled between them. When he fell asleep, they nestled him into his crib and moved as one body toward Allie's bed. Being with Mike was wonderful. He made her feel sexy and empowered and alive.

He went home even earlier this time, but this time she understood, and insisted he leave Brian, his car seat and his overstocked diaper bag with her rather than waking him up. She could see the headline now—"Nanny keeps baby overnight because Dad has an exceptionally early morning." She hoped that take on the situation would fly with the neighbors.

At the appropriate time, she took Brian directly to Mike's apartment and settled him into his usual routine. Even as she played with him on the floor, fed him, bathed him and snuggled him, she couldn't get her mind off Mike.

"You have a great dad," she told Brian when he was crawling toward a covered electrical socket. He paused and turned to look at her.

"You're a lucky boy, and I'm a lucky woman."

"Gah," he said, going right back for the socket.

Allie laughed and scooped him up off the floor. "Exactly. Gah."

Just before dinner, Mike came upstairs. As soon as he walked in, she could tell something was on his mind.

"I have to go to New York next week to talk to the Abernathy company," he said. "Stein called this morning and explained they need to start moving forward if we're going to go through with it."

"New York? Next week?" Allie pulled herself together. She needed to be excited for Mike. "That's wonderful. I can't wait to hear what they have to tell you."

Mike didn't seem all that thrilled. "I'll have to leave early Tuesday morning and come back on Thursday. If they can't explain it to me in two days, either I'm too dumb, or they're too unorganized to franchise the diner."

She smiled at him, hoping he couldn't guess what she was thinking. He'd only be gone for two days, but she'd miss him every second he was away. She needed to get used to it. After all, if he accepted Abernathy's offer and took an active role with the company, he might have to move to New York.

Surely not. He couldn't give up the diner, could he? Wouldn't he always be here while other people ran the franchises? He'd have to be here. He was devoted to his brothers. He must know that Maury would be devastated without him.

The valley depended on him. Mike's Diner was their second kitchen, their spot for birthday and anniversary dinners, their caterer for even more special occasions.

And she needed him to be here when she came home for visits. If a miracle happened, he might still be here waiting for her when she'd done what she had to do.

All this went through her head in a split second before she said, "You know you don't have to worry about anything here. In fact, I can take care of Brian either at my house or here."

"Your house is fine," Mike said. "I appreciate you doing this."

"I love taking care of him," she said, and then, because she couldn't help herself, "You'll keep in touch, won't you?" Hearing the longing in her own voice, she added, trying to sound as if she cared only about the information, "I'll be very interested to know what you're learning."

His gaze met hers and held it. "I'll keep in touch." He said it softly, and then did an abrupt change and said, "Now you'd better stop working, young lady. I can't afford overtime."

Allie laughed, glad the tone had lightened. "I'll punch out on the time clock."

"Or," he said, sounding almost shy, "you might like to stay a while and bring Brian down for dinner."

The look in his eyes told her he'd like her to stay for more than dinner. "Why, thank you," she said. "On the house, I hope?"

"Oh, yes," he said. "Definitely on the house."

OVER THE next few days, Mike's life settled into a pattern. He'd work in the diner during the day and then spend the evening with Allie and Brian. In the back of his mind, he was still worried about holding Allie back from her career plans, or hurting her by neglecting her because he was too busy, but she was so adamant that she understood the risks that he pushed aside his misgivings.

One way or another, their relationship would end in a few months. So he just had to take her word for it that they could "enjoy the moment."

His life only improved when, a few days later, Barney returned to the diner. As was his due, he was greeted with the same fanfare accorded to a visit from the governor. Becky and Colleen had made a handprinted sign out of white butcher's paper to hang over the restaurant doorway. *Barney's Back!* it shouted in huge black letters.

The waitresses hugged him. The interns stammered their names, clearly intimidated by him. A delivery from a florist arrived. It was a cactus plant, and the gift card read You're prickly, but you make a great burger. And it was signed by Elaine Hendricks.

Well, well. This got more interesting every day.

Barney muttered, "Where the heck did they get a cactus plant in Vermont?" But his eyes twinkled even as he went on mumbling and grumbling. He was clearly pleased by the fuss everyone was making over him.

He hadn't lost any of his skills, either. Mike watched him flipping eggs and marveled at his competence. Something settled down inside him, making him feel that life might go back to normal.

Normal plus Brian.

Normal plus Brian and an excited feeling at the mere sight of Allie.

All of which unsettled him an hour later when Allie brought Brian down to meet the legendary Barney. "Well, young man," Barney said, "nice to meet you. Want some eggs and sausage with a biscuit?"

"No," Mike and Allie said in chorus.

"Next year?"

"Maybe."

Daniel's phone call was an ugly bump in an otherwise promising day.

"Of course he'll be fine with Allie," his brother said firmly after Mike had confirmed the rumor that he was going to New York, "as long as both of them go along with you."

Mike took the portable outside, preparing for an argument. "I thought he was supposed to have a stable environment," he reminded Daniel, feeling pretty smug, because for once, he thought he had his brother strung up in his own web.

"He is, but it's more important for him to be with you."

At least Daniel hadn't used the word *bond*. Mike sighed. "You think Brian has to go to New York with me."

"And Allie, so she can take care of him while you're doing business."

Mike had a suspicious feeling about Daniel's insistence. It was one thing for his sister-in-law to be matchmaking, but his own brother? Didn't they understand how impossible the match was on a long-term basis? Still, he couldn't help feeling a rush of heat at the thought of being alone—well, more alone than they'd ever been—in New York with Allie.

"Allie said she'd take care of Brian here. I think that's the best idea."

"I think they should go with you. I bet Allie would jump at the chance. Ask her," Daniel said.

Daniel had a point. Maybe Allie would like to come to New York. He constantly worried about taking advantage of her, and now here was something nice he could do for her. "Okay, okay, I'll ask what she'd like to do."

"You do that," Daniel said, his voice stern. "Be sensitive to her feelings."

Mike knew his brother well enough to know what he was saying. Daniel had figured out there was a change in Mike's relationship with Allie, and he, like everyone else in town, didn't want to see her hurt.

Neither did Mike. "I said I'd ask if she wants to go."

"And if she says yes?"

Mike blew out a sigh. "I'll make sure she has a wonderful time."

Daniel seemed appeased. "Good. Because Allie deserves to be treated well."

"I know." He hung up the phone and went up to the apartment. Allie was reading a book while Brian napped. When he walked in, she gave him a bright smile and said, "Hi, what brings you upstairs?"

Unable to stop himself, he walked over and slipped his arms around her waist. "Daniel says I have to take you and Brian to New York. Naturally, I hate the idea, but I was wondering…"

Her eyes sparkled at him. "I hate the idea, too. I mean, what an imposition to have to go to New York." Then she laughed. "I'd love to. There's so much I could do there with Brian."

"And with me?" Mike kissed her lips lightly, then to stop himself from doing more, he moved back toward the door. "Okay, then, it's a date."

When he got downstairs, he called Richard Stein at Abernathy Foods, who seemed wary. Mike knew why—he assumed Mike was canceling again.

And he sounded so relieved that the opposite was true, that Mike was bringing along an entourage and a freight container of baby supplies, it appeared that he was willing to buy the St. Regis if it would make Mike comfortable.

"We've already booked a suite for you," he crowed.

"Wanted you to feel at home. Three bedrooms? Will that do it?"

"Of—"

"So it's just a matter of two more plane tickets."

"Brian's eight, no, nine months old," Mike said. "He doesn't need a ticket."

Stein chuckled warmly. "My boy," he said, "when I was younger and poorer, my wife and I took several flights handing a squirming baby back and forth, and if you do that, you won't be fit to talk business."

So it was a done deal. In a few days, he and Allie and Brian were off on an adventure. It would be great as long as nobody got hurt by getting too close to each other, then suddenly being torn apart by distance and responsibilities.

A thought hit him hard. Brian could get hurt, too, if Allie, always there, suddenly wasn't.

THE NEW YORK trip settled, Mike returned to the kitchen, feeling optimistic about the upcoming meetings. A few hours later, the squeal of tires caught his attention. Maury, who'd evolved into the star blocker of the football team, arrived at the restaurant late each afternoon with tires screeching. Today they sounded as if they had a life expectancy of about two weeks.

"Problem?" Mike inquired.

"Of course there is," Maury moaned. "The first game's tomorrow night."

"I know *that*," Mike said. "Everybody knows that, and the whole valley's looking for a win. Is that causing you a problem?"

"It means I can't be here at all."

"Of course not," Mike said. "You'll be too sweaty."

When Maury gave him a disgusted look, he added, "We have our interns to help out."

"I know." That one came out as a groan.

Mike had to hide his smile. He had observed that while he'd expected Maury to learn from the interns, Maury seemed to be teaching them.

"Don't worry. Our customers will forgive us anything if you win the game." Mike grinned at him. Maury knew he wasn't hung up on winning, wouldn't be upset if the team tanked.

Turning to his work, his back to Mike, Maury said, "I wish you could be there."

"Me, too." Suddenly a thought occurred to him. "You know," he said slowly. "Maybe I can."

Maury spun. "No way," he said. "You can't. You have to keep an eye on—"

"The interns, yes, but I'm also under orders to do cool things with Brian," Mike said, "and I think he's ready for his first football game." He cleared his throat and deepened his voice. "Can't start too early on those manly things."

On this note, he called Daniel back. After explaining that yes, Allie and Brian were coming with him to New York, so Daniel and Ian could just get off his back, he said, "You guys must be going to Maury's game."

"All of us," Daniel said. "We'll fill up a quarter of the seats."

"I was thinking I might take Brian."

"Good," Daniel said. "Make a jock out of him early."

"No," Mike said, "a loyal Bulldog *fan*."

"You can get away on a Friday night?"

"If I work my tail off getting the prep work done and then try not to think about the final results, because I don't think Maury and I have ever been away from the diner at the same time."

"We'll hold down a couple of rows in the bleachers. Plenty of room for the three of you."

Mike bit his lip. To his family, it was a given that Allie would come along. "I haven't asked Allie yet."

"She'll want to come," Daniel said. "I'm sure of it."

Yeah, he was sure she'd say yes, too, which made him very happy.

ALLIE'S DAY was getting better and better. The glow she felt inside was starting to flame into pure ecstasy. "I'd love to see the game," she said. "And I'm so glad we're going to New York with you. I know you'll be busy, but Brian and I are making plans of our own."

"I hope you don't get bored." Mike sighed.

"Bored in New York? Not possible. There are museums meant for kids, and just walking around the city he'll see and hear so many new things. He'll probably love the subway."

"You'll have to order in from room service," Mike said. "I'm sure you'd be more than welcome to go to dinner with us, but Brian could reduce a top-flight restaurant to a beanery with one well-aimed bread plate."

Allie nodded. "It's a terrifying thought. Don't worry. Brian and I will have a great time."

How could she not have a great time? She'd be with her two favorite men.

"HE CAN'T HAVE popcorn," Mike said nervously before he'd even sat down beside Daniel's youngest foster boy, Nick, to give his shoulders a quick squeeze.

"Hey, Uncle Mike. Hey, Brian."

Soon all of the boys were saying hi to Brian. Ian was

lined up on the bleachers with Daniel's boys and Lilah's son. The oldest, Jason, was flanked by two very pretty girls, his own steady girlfriend and Becky's daughter. Maury had a date! Jason took Brian from Daniel, said something to him that made Brian giggle, then grab Jason's hair with such ferocity it made Mike wince.

The girls were delighted. Jason was wearing a look Mike was familiar with, the look of a teenage boy who's in the middle of something "cute," and he doesn't do "cute."

Maury was in the locker room, of course, undoubtedly wondering not how the game would turn out, but how the beef carbonnade would turn out.

The stadium consisted of a regulation-size field with banks of bleachers on each side. Not a bad seat in the place. Didn't need them with a total of five hundred fans—from both high schools.

Mike glanced around for Allie and saw that she'd slipped away to visit with Lilah. He hoped she'd come back, because he felt an empty spot beside him. And suddenly there she was, saying to Brian, "We're going to sing our national anthem, so put your hand over your heart, like this."

The game began. It was a great night, huge moon, stars everywhere. They hardly needed the field lights. It felt a bit cold, the way autumn should feel, and Mike began to relax, settle in, consider the possibility of having a good time.

He sighed. Sighing brought him closer to Allie. Her thigh touched his lightly. It was nice, soft, and warm. Everything about Allie was nice, soft, and warm.

He realized he was happy. Just think about that.

"Go Maury," Allie cheered.

"Go Maury," he shouted, leaping up. He hadn't been

too out-of-it to see that Maury had just intercepted a pass and returned it for a touchdown.

"Mo," Brian yelled, undoubtedly having no idea why Mike and Allie were yelling, but caught up in the general enthusiasm.

Mike was suddenly filled with an exuberance he didn't know was inside him. "Brian, cheer for Maury! Mo," he yelled.

Allie and Daniel's whole crew stood up too. "Go, Mo," they chanted.

Then a wonderful thing happened. Maury tipped his helmet up, looked into the stands and waved—directly toward Brian, who was shouting "Mo" at the top of his lungs. Maury beamed.

Daniel had his family, but Mike suddenly felt he had his family, too.

It was an amazing sensation.

Chapter Eleven

"Do we have everything?" Mike surveyed the paraphernalia they'd piled to the side of the front door with a combination of amazement and pure horror. Allie had a small suitcase and a carry-on. He had a garment bag and a carry-on. For Brian, they were taking two sizeable suitcases, his folding stroller, a car seat and the inevitable diaper bag.

"We have everything except what we'll realize we've forgotten when it's too late," Allie told him, "and it's too late right now. The car's here." She gazed at it through the window. "I've never gone anywhere in a limousine."

He had, but he'd never tell. "I appreciate the limousine right now," he said. "I'm too tired to drive."

She smiled at him. "Well, the first of the worst parts is over."

"What do you mean, 'the first of the worst parts'?"

"We're packed, we're dressed and Brian, for the moment, is clean and dry."

"Thank the Lord for small blessings," Mike murmured.

"Hear that, Brian?" Allie said, swooping Brian up into her arms. "You're a small blessing."

"When's the next of the worst parts?" Mike asked

her while he loaded his arms with luggage and baby transportation.

"Well, there's the trip to the plane, then waiting for the plane, there's the flight itself, there's the wet diaper, or worse, during the flight, there's settling into the hotel…"

"Okay, okay, you've given me enough to dread for now. I'll take this stuff out and come back for more."

He went through the front door, and the driver rushed toward him. "I'll take those, sir," he said, snatching the two suitcases and the stroller out of Mike's grip. He stashed them in the trunk and said, "Is there more?"

"Oh, yes," Mike sighed.

"Seems you're traveling with a baby." The driver's deadpan expression took on a faint smile. "I've been there, done that."

"Are you relieved they've grown up?" Mike asked him.

"Nope," the man said. "They were easier then."

Mike groaned and led the way up the stairs.

Brian didn't even make it to the airport with a dry diaper. Mike didn't know the Burlington airport had porters, but one mysteriously appeared, pushing a cart, and while the driver loaded the luggage onto it, Allie went inside with Brian and the diaper bag to change him.

Mike, alone now with a full cart, waited for them. He saw Allie and Brian emerge from the women's restroom, Brian flushed and happy, Allie perfectly serene. Did any kid ever have a more unflusterable nanny? Did any kid ever have a more beautiful nanny?

She came up to him, beaming in spite of the fact that her first words were, "I forgot the baby wipes. He's fine for now. I'll add them to my list."

Her list. They'd left home two hours ago and she already had a list.

They checked in and rolled on to security. After Brian's diaper bag had been dissected by the guards, one of them followed Allie's carry-on down the conveyor belt, and giving her a soothing smile, said, "Ma'am, may I take a look inside your bag?"

Naturally they'd want to subject her to a random search. She looked every inch the terrorist, especially when she was holding Brian.

To his surprise, she blushed. "Of course," she said, handed Brian over to Mike, and followed the man to a long counter, where he opened her bag. Mike followed with Brian, the diaper bag, and his shoes dangling from one hand. If Allie needed help, he'd be there for her, and he was there—when the guard delicately pulled from the carry-on something pink and so sheer that Mike had an idea he wasn't supposed to see it yet, but could hardly wait until he did. Preferably on Allie.

"Okay, pal, help me put on my shoes," he said, whisking Brian away before he embarrassed himself.

Allie joined them in a few minutes. "It was my cuff bracelet the machine zeroed in on," she said. "The nice man decided not to arrest me for it." She sounded stiff and formal, as if she were covering her embarrassment, so Mike didn't do what he wanted to—wink at her and suggest she ought to be arrested for that pink whatever-it-was.

"They have to be careful these days," he said, swallowing his smile and saying it with deadly seriousness.

When at last they were on the plane, divided by Brian in the middle seat, Mike got a glimpse of what it would be like to be a newlywed with a baby who woke up crying at inopportune moments. He'd imagined Allie and him engaging in whispered conversation while a perfect baby slept soundly, even if he was between them, but under the current circumstances, there was no way he could get Allie's attention.

The perfect baby wasn't sleeping soundly. Brian wasn't happy in his seat, since the plane looked like a fun place to crawl around in, and she was coaxing him to chew on a gummy-looking teething biscuit. Then she was making faces at him, which finally brought out a smile. The smile led to some embarrassingly loud screeches, which she quieted by singing, "Itsy Bitsy Spider."

He glanced around the cabin. No one was looking at them, probably hoping that if they didn't look at them, they'd go away.

"May I get you something to drink before the flight?" The attendant stood at his side, smiling not at him, but at Brian.

"Allie?" he said.

"I need more coffee," she said.

"Two coffees."

After the flight attendant moved on, Allie was busy again, getting Brian interested in his favorite cloth-bound book, the alphabet book.

"A is for Apple," she hummed, pausing to outline the apple with her fingertip, then point to each letter.

Mike realized he'd have to act like a grown-up and wait his turn.

Mercifully, Brian soared into the air fearlessly, then immediately fell asleep with his head against—

Not Allie's shoulder, but Mike's.

"Look at him." Her voice was soft and loving. "You have no idea what he's been through in the last few hours. Us in a flurry, everything off-schedule, a strange car with a strange man driving the car. A terminal changing room, a waiting room, the plane taking off—"

He hadn't imagined that their whispered conversation would be about Brian, but her smile made him want to tease her. "I went through the same things," he complained. "Nobody's letting me sleep with my head on their shoulder."

"You have to wait until we get to the hotel," she said sternly.

"It won't be easy."

She flushed, looking young and innocent, which she was. His eyes drifted over her lovely face. She was innocent of the evil in the world. Innocent about hard times, selfish parents. He hoped she'd never lose that innocence, she'd never know sadness or fear. He'd never tell her about his own unhappiness, his loneliness, his feeling of not being loved that had made him lash out at the world to get attention. Or about the knots that twisted in his stomach at the slightest uncertainty. He wanted her to buy the person he appeared to be: cheerful, a regular stand-up guy, happy-go-lucky—at least until Brian came along—cool about everything, totally secure.

A strong man, which she thought he was. When, in fact, he was a ripe tomato, ready to burst at the slightest blow, just as the tomato at Mayhew's Market had been.

As any gentleman would do, he engaged her in small talk, the news, national rather than LaRocque, small details about the restaurant and bigger details about Brian. Just as their conversation was about to turn personal, the pilot announced, "We're starting our descent into JFK…"

Brian woke up, screaming, Allie swiftly pulled a

bottle out of the diaper bag and stuck it in his mouth, informing Mike that his ears probably hurt and sucking would help him get through it, and life was back to what he was starting to think of as normal—minus a place where he could bring down his blood pressure by cooking.

They landed. Mike had no problem finding their driver. Hard to miss your own name on a sandwich board the man wore around his neck.

"Have you checked luggage, Mr. Foster?" the man said, then took a look at Brian and said, "Yes, of course you have."

Starting toward the baggage carousel, Allie said calmly, "Brian needs to be changed. Where shall I meet you?"

She left with Brian and the ever-present diaper bag while Mike and the driver waited for the luggage. "You have kids?" Mike asked him.

"Seven."

Mike's head reeled. "So you understand car seats and gigantic suitcases for a single twenty-four-pounder…"

"Yep."

"Any babies now?"

"Nope."

"Are you relieved that they've grown up?"

"Nope. They were easier then."

It was the second time today he'd gotten the same bad news. He was feeling glum when Allie returned at last with Brian, who studied the driver and seemed to give him a grudging approval, although he clung to Allie, then held out his arms for his personal parking space, Mike's left hip.

At last, when the driver had retrieved the car, had gone through an endless drill to pick them up outside the terminal, crammed the trunk to its maximum capacity and wrestled the car seat into its moorings, they were on their way to the hotel. It was early afternoon, and Mike felt as if he'd fought a war singlehandedly and deserved six weeks of rest and rehabilitation. Allie, on the other hand, was pointing out buildings on the New York skyline to Brian.

Mike thought about her energy and his lack of it. He was a healthy, relatively young man. He could manage a full day at the restaurant, occasionally a night of getting started on a catering job, a day at the restaurant followed by the catering job itself, and not feel the least bit tired.

Now he was exhausted. It must have something to do with having a kid, but he was too tired to figure out what that something was.

They arrived at the hotel, which was like a palace. As they checked in, the clerk said, "We've put you in the Lucerne Suite," he said, "very comfortable, and we hope you'll feel at home there."

It wasn't until they were alone in the suite that Mike felt the full impact of the situation. He and Allie were away from LaRocque, where everybody knew everything about everybody else. It would be the first real privacy they'd ever had. He had no idea what these meetings with Abernathy would entail. He had no idea what privacy with Allie would do to his logical thinking. He just hoped he was up to it all.

ALLIE STARED disbelievingly at their home away from home. "This is amazing," she said. "The last time I was in New York, I stayed in a room the width of a double bed and two nightstands. You couldn't have the closet door and the bathroom door open at the same time."

Mike grinned at her. "Want to explore?"

They wandered through the suite. The living room was larger than Mrs. Langston's. Three bedrooms, two baths, small kitchen, and all of it beautifully furnished and decorated. "A starter home," she said. "For a wealthy young couple, that is."

Mike gave her a quick kiss. "I'd like to stick around, but I have to get to the Abernathy building in a hurry." He grabbed his suitcase and vanished into one of the bedrooms.

She stood in the living room holding Brian and wondering where to start. By feeding him, of course. One look at the splendid chintz-covered armchairs in the living room motivated her to drag one of the wooden dining chairs that surrounded a small table into the kitchen, and there she fed Brian, grateful that her shirt was washable.

Mike came out of the bedroom while she was on her hands and knees mopping up puréed green beans from the marble floor. She looked up and gasped, then stood to take him in from head to toe. "I've never seen you in a suit," she said.

He looked embarrassed. "Bought it for Daniel's wedding."

He was a vision in the navy suit. It hung perfectly from his broad shoulders, and the trousers, sharply creased, outlined his narrow hips in a way that stirred her blood.

"You look gorgeous."

That seemed to embarrass him more. "Okay, gotta go. Will you and Brian be okay?"

If I can stop thinking about you. "Of course." Brian supported her by burbling assurance from the car seat she'd strapped him into while she cleaned up.

"Remember your new best friend, room service," he reminded her. "I feel bad about not coming back for dinner."

"A business dinner is important. The conversation will be less intense, more casual. You may learn more there than you will in their offices." She straightened his tie.

"You think they'll invite me to play golf?"

She laughed. "Eventually they will. Probably not on this trip." She tweaked the handkerchief in his breast pocket.

"Good, because I don't play golf. Bye, Brian," he said, and gave the baby a kiss on the top of his head.

He held out his arms to gather Allie close, but she jumped back. "Green beans don't match your outfit," she said, pointing to her shirt.

Wearing a wry smile, he leaned over to give her a kiss, physically distant, maybe, but a lovely kiss nonetheless. "Wish me luck," he said.

"Luck," she whispered, her lips lingering on his. "It'll go great."

With a look she hoped was a longing one, he left.

How far he'd come since the morning he went down to the diner without kissing Brian or even telling him goodbye. She smiled. He wouldn't be able to resist loving Brian like his own son.

Her smile faded. She hoped she could resist loving Mike just as much.

Remembering why she was here, she said, "Okay, Brian, a quick change and cleanup, and then we'll take a walk! New York, New York, it's a wonderful town," she sang, and Brian chuckled.

"MIKE!"

Richard Stein seemed happy to see him. *Thrilled*

would be a better word, even *ecstatic.* "Come right in," he said. "We'll have lunch and then get to work. Are your accommodations adequate?"

"Very pleasant," Mike said, restraining himself from gushing.

"And the trip went well?"

Stein really didn't want to hear cute baby stories, Mike was certain, so he said, "Yes, quite well, thank you," and he smiled, graciously he hoped.

Lunch met his standards and then some. Abernathy Foods either had its own star chef or an excellent caterer. Six of them sat at the table, and they began giving him an overview of the company even before the snails were served. After lunch they really got down to business, and he began to long for Allie to be sitting at his side, her calm attitude and good judgment giving him strength.

ALLIE WALKED Brian uptown to Central Park. His first treat was a trip to the most famous toy store in the world. He was fascinated by the singing clock, which was a good thing because there was no way he could grab it.

It was the only thing he couldn't grab. She centered the stroller in each aisle, hoping the impatient shoppers who scooted around her understood that the alternative would be a floor covered with every toy Brian could reach.

He wasn't misbehaving. He was smart, curious, just the way a baby should be. "Look at the polar bear, Brian," she said when they passed a display of stuffed toys. Taking a chance, she handed it to him. He hugged it, and when he didn't want to let go, she bought it for him.

The price was appalling. She couldn't afford it, but the ruckus Brian made when she had to take it away from him so the clerk could scan the tag made the purchase seem like nothing in comparison.

"So that's the toy store," she said, whisking him out the door. "Now let's go to the zoo!"

She was as fascinated by the zoo as Brian was. It was a beautiful, sunny fall day, the kind that lifted her spirits, made everything look golden. Even as she talked to Brian, telling him the name of each animal, she was thinking about Mike, what confusing or disturbing facts and conditions were being thrown at him, how he was handling it.

On the outside, she was sure he was handling it in a businesslike way, just as he managed the diner, always cheerful, always with a twinkle in his eye. But why had she always wondered if he felt the same way inside? Was it some vibe thrumming from him that she picked up on when nobody else seemed to?

She was probably just wrong. "Look, Brian," she said, "polar bears just like yours, but lots, lots bigger!"

They continued their stroll through the zoo, at last ending up at the aviary. It contained birds of all species, birds from dozens of countries, and yet they got along together.

She realized something about herself she'd never thought of. She was like these birds. She didn't have to be separated from anyone. She relished contact with any human foible, weakness or need, with no agenda except to make the people with those problems feel better.

Help people feel better. That was what she'd always wanted to do, and that was what she would do, but not as a doctor, as a therapist.

The feeling that came over her was one of pure joy. She'd thought psychology was a maybe, but now she knew it was what she'd wanted to do. At last, she'd made her career decision. She didn't have to worry anymore. About many other things, but not that. Her heart lightened, and she felt a burst of energy. "Brian," she said with refreshed enthusiasm, "That's a parrot. Par-rot, and that's a—"

MIKE FELT as if his brain had turned into a calculator. Abernathy Foods had made an offer that any sensible man couldn't refuse. But he didn't know the conditions yet.

He couldn't wait to get back to the St. Regis. His guess was that Brian was already in bed and asleep, but with any luck, Allie would still be awake, because he needed someone to talk to in the worst way. Not Daniel or Ian. The person he wanted to talk to was Allie.

He unlocked the door to the suite and saw her sitting on the sofa, her feet curled up under her, wearing something pink and sheer, the scrap of fabric the security guard had plucked out of her carry-on, with an equally sheer robe over it. As always, she was reading, and when she saw him, she flung the book aside and stood up slowly. "How were the meetings?" she asked.

Mike felt the air whoosh out of his lungs. "Good."

She moved toward him, the sheer gown and robe revealing more than they concealed. "Tell me what happened."

"I can't," he admitted when she stood close to him. "All the blood has left my brain."

"Oh, really?"

He slipped his arms around her waist. "Mmm. Yes. Maybe later I can remember, but right now—"

Then he kissed her.

BRIAN'S COMPLAINING cries woke Allie the next morning. She reluctantly climbed out of the warm bed, pulled on sweatpants and a T-shirt, then padded to the baby's room. "Hi, sweetie."

Brian smiled at her and talked up a storm while she changed him, then went into the kitchen. She sat him in his car seat and said, "What's for breakfast?"

"I'll have the puréed apricots."

She spun to see Mike standing in the doorway.

He was wearing a pair of jeans low on his hips. The sight of him made her heartbeat pick up. "Puréed apricots? Without turning them into an apricot soufflé?" she asked him.

He gave her a slow, sexy smile. "I'm way too distracted to make a soufflé," he said, "And it's a great feeling. How about you?"

"I'd never attempt a soufflé, and certainly not now," she said, "not with you looking at me that way." She moved toward him, but Brian indicated that she'd better come back at once.

"He's hungry," Allie said, deserting Mike reluctantly.

"So am I. For food, among other things. We'll order from room service. My first meeting isn't until nine."

Allie glanced at the clock. Babies certainly got your days going early.

"I'll make that first cup of coffee right now," he told her. "I'd rather serve it to you in bed," and his eyes roamed over her as he spoke, "but this will have to do. You want to call room service while I feed Brian, or the other way around?"

"I'm on phone duty," she said, giving him a mischievous smile. Watching him spoon apricots into the baby's mouth while she placed their order, she realized she'd never felt this good, this fulfilled. She couldn't ever remember feeling this—blissful. She wasn't just happy, she was content. Content with what she was doing, content with the way her life was going.

The way it was going right this minute. With a sinking feeling, she realized it was already too late, that she loved them both, loved Mike passionately, loved Brian as if he were her own child. She couldn't imagine not being with them every day.

Impulsively she said, "I'm so happy, Mike."

He smiled at her. "It's good to be happy."

She suddenly felt shy, but she forged ahead. "I mean I'm happy right now, I like my life, I like what I'm doing. I don't want anything to change." She took a deep breath. "But yesterday I decided for sure what I wanted to study. Psychology. I want to be a clinical psychologist if I can get through the Ph.D. program."

His face lit up, and his eyes sparkled. "It's just what you should do. I want to get up and hug you, but…" He gestured to Brian, to his fruit-stained shirt. "Just you wait." His smile was filled with promise.

Promise of what? Promise to respect her if she went back to school? Promise to wait for her until she finished her education? "I realize," she rushed on, "that I could help you with Brian until he's a bit older and then start the program…" *But…* But what if she settled in contentedly just as her mother said she might and didn't go back to school, ever?

She glanced at Mike. He'd drawn his eyebrows together ever so slightly, so that he looked worried, or disapproving, maybe. It made her want to throw her arms around him, spilled baby food and all, and tell him that no matter what happened, she loved him. But with that expression on his face, she couldn't tell him what was in her heart.

His face cleared as suddenly as it had clouded over. "We'll talk about it tonight. Right now, I have to clean up this young man before our breakfast gets here. Right, Brian?" He lifted the baby high into the air, making him shriek happily and wave his hands.

He was Mike as usual, cheerful, smiling, starting his day with enthusiasm. She stood in the kitchen for a moment, thinking about his growing and building relationship with Brian, and about her increasing love for both of them.

It was all about Brian, really, wasn't it? Brian deserved a focused father. He didn't deserve an often-absent—she could hardly bear to think the word—mother.

She knew what she had to do, even if it broke her heart.

Chapter Twelve

Even though Allie was worried sick about the conversation she would have with Mike that night, she knew exactly how to entertain Brian today. The question was how to get there. Consulting a transportation map, she walked him to the closest subway station and peered down into it.

Stairs. Tons of stairs. She looked doubtfully at Brian's stroller and decided his first subway experience would have to wait until he was walking.

"But *I* can walk," she told Brian, and they did, thirty blocks north to the Museum of Natural History.

Brian was enthralled by the dinosaurs, the huge whale model suspended from the ceiling entranced him, and the grizzly bear made him say, "Ohhh." At first, Allie gave him her complete attention, but at some point, she felt her thoughts drifting. It wasn't the way a nanny should behave, but in the cool dimness of one of the display rooms, she felt all her concerns descend on her as heavily as if the whale had dropped from the ceiling right on top of her. Just yesterday, she'd felt her load had lightened.

It was mid October, which left her ten weeks to worry about whether she was doing the right thing, to change her mind if she wanted to. The look on Mike's face this morning—what did it mean? Was he hoping she'd stay? Or go, leaving him to concentrate on Brian and the restaurant, in that order.

But at that moment, she was a nanny, not a woman struggling to choose between love and a career. She peered around the stroller at Brian. "Hey, Brian, is this enough natural history for you today?" His head had lolled to one side and his eyes were droopy. Feeling very tired, she left the museum and hailed a cab.

In the luxurious suite, she fed and changed Brian, looked without interest at the room-service menu, then ordered the closest thing to a grilled cheese sandwich she could find.

While Brian slept, she finished the book she'd been reading, a study of various mental conditions, wondering again if she was doing the right thing or ruining her life forever.

MIKE TRIED HARD to listen to what Richard Stein and his colleagues were saying. "Six franchises to start with," blah, blah, blah, "…not economically viable to have a different special each night, so we were thinking about a blue plate special for each night of the week," yada, yada, yada.

He could hear the words, he was aware that although the plan made economic sense, he didn't like it much, but his mind was on Allie.

She'd thrown him a curve this morning, made him wonder what she really wanted to do. When she suggested she didn't have to go back to school immediately, he should have leapt at the chance she was handing him on a velvet pillow—and handed back that same pillow with an engagement ring on it.

Still, he'd heard the uncertainty in her voice. She

didn't want to be, and he didn't want her to be, one of those people who'd grown up in the valley and couldn't imagine going beyond it. It was different for him. The valley was his resting place from the fights he'd had with the world outside the valley.

Maybe, just maybe, there was a way for each of them to...

"How does this sound so far?" Stein asked him.

"Like something that will take a lot of thought," Mike said, knowing he wasn't talking about franchising, but about Allie.

After the meeting ended, he walked back to the hotel. He couldn't wait to talk to her about the information he'd gleaned. He was so conflicted about what he wanted to do with the diner that only Allie could straighten him out.

Was he using her, or was it just that he depended on her? Too much, maybe. He and Brian both did. But franchising was an important issue, wasn't it? He'd kiss her, hug her, snuggle her against him, and after...well, after, she'd be happy to help him weigh the pros against the cons.

It occurred to him that he could return the favor, help her sort out the pros and cons of going back to school, like when and how to...

How to. Yes! He walked faster. There were ways for Allie to go back to school and still be a part of his and Brian's life. Ideas hummed through his head. With every step his heart felt lighter. He'd tell her all about it, even before they talked about his day at Abernathy.

He stepped into the suite intending to do just that, but instead of finding Allie alone, he found her holding Brian.

"He's teething," she said, looking down affectionately

at the fussy boy grinding his fists into his mouth. "We had some medicine delivered, and I was about to rub it on his gums."

The conversation would have to boil inside him until the right moment presented itself. He took off his suit jacket, sat beside her, and took Brian onto his lap. She squeezed a small amount of the medicine onto her fingertip and approached Brian's mouth with it.

He wailed, turned away from her and buried his head under Mike's arm. As Mike was about to offer Brian's mouth for medication whether he liked it or not, she said, "Look, Brian, look at Allie."

Brian quieted down and took a peek. Allie rubbed her fingertip over her own gums. "Ooh, that feels so good," she crooned. "It's cool, it tastes pretty good… you know, I think I'll just rub in some more since you're not interested."

Brian sat up and stared at her, pressing down hard on another one of those teething biscuits. "Yum, yum," she said in a singsong voice. "I might have to use all of it, Brian, because it's so nice."

It wasn't long before Brian reached out for the tube. Allie said, "I guess I could let you have some, too, if you really want it. Open your mouth and close your eyes and you will get a big surprise."

Of course Brian didn't understand the directions, but he let her take the cookie away from him and open his mouth just enough to rub the gel on his gums, ever so gently, ever so lightly. Talking to him softly, she massaged and massaged until Mike felt the baby begin to droop in his lap.

"HE'S ALMOST asleep," she whispered, gazing at Brian's closed eyes, at Mike holding Brian with such assurance, feeling her heart expand with love for both of them.

Mike nodded. "You did it. You made Brian think that salve was the next best thing to ice cream. Now that's good psychology. It's what you were meant to do."

"I hope so." Or was she meant to be Mike's wife, Brian's mother? Her heart pounded loudly in her chest. "Mike," she said, "I want to hear all about your day." She paused. "And talk about some other things, too."

"I'll put this boy to bed," Mike said abruptly, "and then we can talk."

Mike put Brian into his crib and hung around long enough to be sure he was still asleep. He'd been so excited by finding possible solutions to his and Allie's situation, but when Allie said *she* wanted to talk to *him,* something about her tone gave him a bad feeling.

WHEN HE WENT back to the living room, Allie was curled on the couch, looking so desirable that he remembered at once that Brian had scotched the hugging and kissing part of his homecoming. He was about to reach out for her, about to spill out all his thoughts about their future together, when she said in an all-too-practical tone, "What happened today?"

He guessed he'd have to start with the business side of the conversation. He sat beside her, wishing her curled-up legs weren't keeping him from sitting closer. "They want to make some big changes, and I'm not sure I like them. It's a catch-22. The diner is unique, but what makes it unique makes it hard to franchise."

Allie nodded. "You've put your own stamp on the diner. Without you right there in the kitchen or talking to the customers, it won't be the same. But it could still be good."

He sighed and leaned back against the cushions. "They're offering me so much money. I'd be rich. My family would be rich."

As he'd expected, Allie didn't seem impressed by that. "If that would make you happy, you should consider the offer."

He closed his eyes. "Happy to have done something for my brothers, but personally I might be miserable. Abernathy would like me to move to New York and work for them to replicate our menu. Specials, yes, but more like Monday Pot Roast and Tuesday Lasagna. Everything we offer would be by formula—a hamburger would be six ounces of beef, an inch and a quarter thick, and so on. I'd like to have some influence on those decisions, but—" he leaned toward her "—I'm not moving to New York. Allie—"

"Mike," she interrupted him, no longer looking or sounding practical, "If you want to move to New York, you should. Because I've made a difficult decision. You'll never know how difficult." Her eyes filled with tears.

Mike drew back a little. It took all his self-control to keep his voice steady. "Go on."

"The first thing I have to tell you is…is that I love you."

"I love you, too. With all my heart. And I was thinking—"

"No, wait. Let me finish." Her gaze pleaded with him to understand. "I've realized love isn't all passion and romance. It's doing the best thing for the person you love."

"Allie, the best thing—"

"The best thing—" and her voice broke "—is for you to be free to become a real father to Brian, to be free to make this deal with Abernathy without having me to think about. I'm getting out of your life, Mike, so we can both do what's best for us." A sob escaped her. "I don't want it to be this way, but it has to. Please understand. I love Brian, too, so very much, and I think he loves me. But he needs permanence in his life. That's you, Mike, unencumbered and showering all your love on him." She paused, tears streaming down her face. "If you're still there when I've finished what I have to do, I hope we can start all over again."

Ice formed over his heart, filled his veins. "I don't want it to be this way, either, but I know you're right." He gazed into her eyes. "As soon as we get back to LaRocque, I'll find a new nanny."

She seemed to crumple. Slowly she stood and walked away—to the bedroom next to Brian's rather than the one they'd shared.

Mike stayed on the sofa, feeling as if his life had ended.

ALLIE MADE A tour of Mrs. Langston's house, looking for anything she might have forgotten, then went back to the living room, where her mother waited to say goodbye.

"I'm proud of you, honey. I know it wasn't an easy decision," Elaine said. "But getting a doctorate in psychology is a *good* decision. An adult decision. You won't regret it."

Allie nodded absently. She was going to miss this house. A lot. Just like she was going to miss this town. And the people. And…

Mike and Brian.

"In Burlington, you won't be as distracted as if you stayed here," Elaine went on, "surrounded by memories. Being away will ease the hurt a little."

Allie felt that nothing could ever dull the pain. "I just hope I can get into the doctoral program," she said, feeling as dull as her voice. She closed her second suitcase and placed it near the doorway.

"I'm confident they'll accept you." Elaine's voice was reassuring. "And you're so lucky you can stay in Suzy's apartment until you find your own place to settle into."

Again, Allie nodded. Yes, she was lucky. Lucky Suzy was spending the fall semester doing some special coursework in Boston. Lucky that she would be able to talk to professors, department heads and campus counselors to get an even better idea of what she was getting into.

She was just overflowing with luck these days.

"Of course, I'll miss you, but you'll be back soon for the benefit." Her mother folded an afghan and laid it over the back of Allie's special wing chair.

The benefit. The details of the dinner were in perfect order, but could she bear to go to it? To see Mike so soon? "I'm not sure if I'll come back, Mom. We'll see."

Her mother raised a cautionary hand. "You can't miss it. I don't know what exactly happened between you and Mike, but you still have to come to the benefit, Allie. You have a responsibility to see it through to the end."

Her mother's expression was stern, and she was using the same voice she'd used when Allie had been small and had tracked mud into the house.

But her mother didn't understand. Right now, she couldn't imagine being in a room with Mike without bursting into tears. A sobbing woman wouldn't exactly help them raise money for the foster-care center.

Just as she realized the bitterness in her thoughts, her mother said, "Lemonade."

Allie stared at her.

"Lemonade," her mother said again. "You've been handed a bag of lemons, Allie. You have a choice. You can either let them turn you sour and bitter or—"

"I can make lemonade," Allie said.

Her mother patted her cheek. "Yes, exactly. So go make lemonade."

Chapter Thirteen

"We have to start sometime," Mike told Brian. He stood at the head of the stairs with Brian on his hip, the diaper bag slung around his neck and the playpen dangling from his right hand.

He'd never fallen down the stairs, but if he ever did, it would be this morning. He couldn't leave Brian alone while he took the playpen down, so he'd have to do it the other way around.

"Would you mind bringing the playpen down from the head of the stairs?" he asked an intern on morning duty.

The intern glanced at Brian, then looked nervously back at the roux he'd been stirring. "You have about thirty seconds before it burns," Mike said, "so hurry."

The intern darted away and darted right back with the playpen. Mike hauled it into his office and put Brian in it with a stacking toy and the stuffed rabbit.

Just looking at the rabbit Allie had bought for Brian made him sad.

He got to work, keeping the door to his office open so he had a clear view of Brian. Fifteen minutes of work, and Brian began to whimper. He didn't need a diaper change, Mike discovered. He didn't want conversation, either, because Mike tried and got smacked on the hand with the rabbit.

He knew what was wrong. Brian was bored. He didn't want to spend his life playing in a playpen. By now, Allie would have been on the floor with him upstairs, joining him in his games. Then she'd dress him for their first walk of the day.

Mike ached when he thought about Allie, so he just wouldn't think about her. "Hang on," he told Brian. "If I can just make a little more progress here, we'll do something fun."

Brian scowled, but he busied himself with two wooden spoons Mike had given him.

With the benefit tomorrow night and somehow keeping the diner open, Mike was strapped for time. Since Allie had left, he'd felt as if he were plodding through molasses. No, he wasn't going to think about Allie. He was going to think about—

His gaze moved in an arc when the wooden spoons flew past him and landed an amazing distance from the playpen. Brian screwed up his face and started to cry. Mike picked him up. "Hey," he said, "don't tell me you don't want to be in the restaurant business."

He bounced Brian up and down. He was afraid to take him close to the kitchen equipment, so he pointed. "See Barney?" he said. "See how much fun he's having flipping those pancakes?"

Brian buried his face in Mike's shirt and howled.

"Let me take him a minute," Colleen said, putting down the breakfast order she was about to take out.

He handed Brian over and took the order out himself. In the background, he could hear Brian's howls turning into screams, so he dashed back into the office.

"Maybe he's sick," he said, but Brian's forehead

was cool even though his face was hot and red from crying.

"He's missing Allie," Colleen said pointedly, and handed Brian back to Mike.

She didn't have to tell him. He felt like howling, too.

At nine o'clock, when everybody in the kitchen and half the customers had held Brian for awhile, he gave up.

"Brian," he said persuasively, "how about a walk?"

Brian stopped throwing the rabbit out of the playpen for Becky to put back in.

"Okay, let's do it. Get as far with this as you can," he told the intern who'd been prepping the dinner special. "I'll be back in a while."

The phone rang. Colleen answered it, and Mike was almost out the door when she rushed after him, the portable in her hand. "This sounds important."

Impatiently, juggling Brian on his hip, he took the phone. "Earl Ritter here," the voice said.

"Mr. Ritter. Hey, could I call you back? I have an unhappy boy here—"

"In a minute," Ritter said. "I'm at Evan's house going through his papers, as I was instructed to do, and found a letter to you. Perhaps he meant to include it with the will. I'll send it to you."

Just what he needed right now. A note from his father. What could the man do that he hadn't already done?

He had to know, as soon as possible, get it over with. "Would you fax the letter to me?" Mike asked as Brian began to squirm and yell at the same time.

"Of course. If you don't mind my opening it."

"Open it. Fax it. Here's the number."

He handed the phone back to Colleen, then took a

long, long look at Brian, his father's child, his half-brother. His son. He couldn't wait for the fax, although he wanted to. He needed to get Brian calmed down. He took the baby upstairs, changed him, dressed him for the outdoors and, motivated by Brian's obvious distress, began to hurry.

With Brian in the stroller, he set off at a brisk pace. Peering down to see how the boy was doing, he saw that while he wasn't crying, he didn't look happy, either.

He was doing the best he could, Mike told himself. He was taking time away from his work to walk a fussy child, he was trying to entertain him, he hadn't lost his temper, and he hadn't cut himself the last time Brian began shrieking. He had a new burden on his shoulders—that note from Evan—and still he was doing what it took to make Brian happy. What more could anyone ask of him?

Plenty, he told himself a few minutes later when Brian began whimpering again. Maybe the thing to do was to tell him what had happened and why he should be happy for Allie. It would be a heck of a lot better than going on saying it to himself. He went across the street and into the town square, found a bench in a sun-dappled spot beneath some trees, sat down and pulled the stroller close to him.

"Here's the deal, Brian. You love Allie and she loves you." *She loves me, too. She told me she loves me. She wouldn't have made love with me if she didn't, and heaven help me, I love her more than my own life, I want her, I need her.*

Brian's eyes had opened wide at the sound of Allie's name. "But she needs more out of life than being a nanny. She's smart, Brian, really smart. She needs a career. She needs the self-satisfaction of knowing she's helping more people than just us. Unhappy people who will feel better after they talk to her."

Just the way I do. And I need to talk to her now, need her with me when I read that letter.

Brian's face screwed up. "I know, I know," Mike said quickly. "You're unhappy, too, and I admit it, kiddo, I'm not happy myself, but we can't ask Allie to come back and save us. She has her own work to do."

Brian frowned deeply, and Mike began to feel desperate. "We have to let her do it," he insisted. "Maybe someday she can come back, when she's a full-fledged psychologist. Maybe she'll decide to set up an office in town and live with us. Who knows? Whaddaya think about that, huh?"

Nothing good, it was clear. He leaned closer to the boy, who instantly grabbed the points of his collar with both hands and tugged, putting all his strength into it, and glared ferociously at Mike.

"You think I should have tried harder? You think I should have figured out a way for her to stay with us and still have a professional life? You think I should have told her we'd wait for her, we'd be grateful for any time she could give us?"

Still glaring, still keeping a stranglehold grip on Mike's collar, Brian yelled, "Da."

Mike felt stunned. "Did you just say Da?" Did he dare to hope? "You said Dad?"

Without thinking, he reached into his pocket for his cell and punched in Allie's number. She answered, her voice as beautiful, as musical, as appealing as ever.

"Brian just said Da," he blurted out. Realizing what he'd done, he pushed the End button with his thumb, then turned the phone off.

His first thought had been to call Allie. Of course.

She was the first person he wanted to know that this stupendous thing had happened. Even before he told Daniel or Ian.

Brian was trying to take the phone away from him, protesting, babbling and still glaring at Mike. Mike gazed at him, feeling something warm and bubbly rise up inside, stirring his heart, tightening his throat, making his eyes feel hot.

All at once, he knew what it was. He was consumed with love for this determined child, the love he hadn't wanted to admit to himself until now. He no longer cared why his father had left Brian to him, he cared only that Evan had done it, and for that, Mike was grateful. Loving Brian had dimmed his resentment toward his father. He could read that letter, and whatever it said, he could survive it. He could leave that dark side of himself behind, forever.

"That's right, Brian. I'm your dad." He picked up his baby and hugged him close. One day he'd have to explain to Brian that they were brothers, but for now, he was his son. Mike loved him and wanted Brian to love him in return. He wanted Brian to have the best life any boy could have. He didn't even care if Brian learned to cook. He just wanted him to be happy.

And he loved Allie. God, how he loved Allie. And she loved him, and Brian… What had he been thinking?

"You're right," he said to Brian, putting him back into the stroller. "I've been a complete idiot."

Brian, having no idea what he was talking about, looked up at him and smiled. Mike grabbed the handles of the stroller and ran to the Hendricks's house, with Brian shrieking, this time in delight.

Elaine Hendricks wasn't at home, or if she was, she

wasn't letting him in. Disappointed, he said to Brian, "At least we tried."

Now he didn't feel like running. His feet felt like lead as he went back to the diner. "We'll find Allie eventually," he assured Brian. "It won't be long before I run into Elaine on the street, or maybe she'll come to lunch."

Back in the diner, he went directly to his office, where the fax from Ritter caught his eye. He put the cover sheet behind the note—the original had been handwritten— and began to read.

Dear Mike:

I write this letter knowing you may tear it up without reading it, and I wouldn't blame you. When Brian was born, when I saw how much Celine loved him, how much time she spent with him, how she thought of our nanny as a babysitter for when she had to go out, not as a replacement mother, I realized how empty of affection your childhood was, and I felt ashamed.

Mike's eyes widened. What was this?

I hired a private investigator, found out where you were and learned what you'd accomplished in spite of the lonely childhood your mother and I gave you. I learned that you created your own family with two fine men, Daniel and Ian, a family who love and care about each other. I felt such pride in the man who'd always been inside you, a strong man with a good heart, and again I felt that shame, shame that I hadn't worked hard to bring that out

in you when you were just a boy. Your life would
have been so different.

It is for all these reasons that I'm appoint-
ing you guardian of Brian in the unlikely event of
Celine's and my death. Somehow, in spite of your
experience with neglectful parents, you've learned
to love and care, and if I can't love and care for
Brian, I trust you to do for him what I should have
done for you.

Please forgive me.

Your father,

Evan Howard

Stunned, Mike read the letter again. "A person he
trusted," Lilah had said, and he'd laughed at her. Hot,
burning tears blurred the words he stared at.

Hearing a commotion in the kitchen, he wiped his
eyes, put down the fax and picked up Brian, who'd begun
to fuss again, from his playpen. Together, they went out
to see what was going on.

What was going on was Barney, smiling sheepishly,
with Elaine Hendricks, who was holding her left hand to
Colleen and Becky while they shrieked with delight.

"Look at her ring," Becky crowed. "She and Barney
are getting married."

Mike glanced at the ring. "Very nice. Congratula-
tions, Barney. Elaine, where's Allie?"

The kitchen fell into silence. Elaine took back her
hand and stared at him. "She's...she's in Burlington,"
she said at last.

"Where in Burlington?"

"She didn't want anybody to know where she was
until she got things settled." Elaine looked longingly at
Brian, who reached out for her.

"I can't wait until she gets things settled," he said, "I have to talk to her *now*. In person."

"I promised her," Elaine said, pleading with him to understand. "She has to have time alone to work things out."

"Elaine," Mike said, calming down enough to look her straight in the eyes, "do *you* want me to find Allie?"

Her gaze dropped to the kitchen floor. Then she looked back at Mike and put her finger to her lips. Reaching for one of his order pads, she scribbled on it and handed it to him.

On it was an address.

Mike gazed at her. "I get it," he said softly. "You didn't tell me." He threw his arms around her and hugged her, because, after all, she was going to be his mother-in-law, sooner, he hoped, rather than later.

"I have to leave," he told his surprised staff. "We may be serving scrambled eggs at the benefit tomorrow night, but I have to leave."

A few minutes later, he and Brian were in the car heading for the freeway, where he drove as fast as he thought fathers were allowed to—slightly *under* the speed limit.

ALLIE STARED at her phone. Mike had called her. But he'd hung up after telling her what Brian had done.

Hoping he'd just lost service, she called him back, but got his voice mail. He didn't want to talk to her. He might have called her by accident—had her number programmed and pushed the wrong button, that it was Daniel, not she, with whom he wanted to share the big news.

She missed them so much she hurt. Could she stand to see them tomorrow night at the benefit?

For the past several hours, she'd been alternating among crying, filling out endless application forms and blotting the tears off the application forms. She stood to pour another cup of tea and caught a glimpse of herself in the mirror over the sink. She was a wreck, her hair hanging lank and uncombed, no makeup and wearing the gray sweatsuit from her high-school days, her comfort symbol. *I've turned into a slob.*

But who did she have to dress up for?

Was she doing the right thing in going back to school? Mike had left her no other choice, had he? With each bit of information she'd gathered, she'd been more sure of her career choice, and less sure she could stand being away from Mike for even another hour, much less the time her coursework and training would take. But it would be worth it, she told herself stubbornly. And then immediately she thought, "Worth leaving Mike and Brian?"

And she went back to crying.

The banging on the door startled her. Swiping madly at her eyes, she opened it. On the stoop stood Mike, Brian squirming on his hip, smiling, burbling and trying to reach out for her.

She wouldn't let herself reach for him. "Mike? What are you doing here?"

"We're here to stay," Mike said, barging through the door, "if you can love a man as stupid as I am." He faced her. His eyes were wild, and she wondered if he realized he was still wearing his white chef's jacket.

She was too shocked to speak. She could only stare at him.

"I was an idiot to let you walk out on me," he said. "I sat there and let you do it because I was afraid to be any closer to you, afraid my wall would fall down—"

"Your wall? Mike, what are you talking about?" Had she hurt him so much he'd lost his mind?

"I've lied to you, to everybody in the valley. Brian isn't the child of an old friend. He's my father's child. I haven't told you who I really am."

She could only listen silently as the story spilled out of him, his childhood, his time in juvenile detention, his bond with Daniel and Ian. "They're the only people I trust, the only people I haven't built walls against. But the wall I'd built between you and me, well, I felt it starting to crumble—until you said you didn't want to be with me anymore. My pride took over. I refused to beg you for love."

"Oh, Mike—" Tears overflowed her eyes. She had made the wrong decision. She knew that now, from her own misery and his. "You have my love. More love than you've ever had in your life. But I didn't know how we could work this out. It wouldn't be good for Brian to have me popping in and out of his life. Not good for us, either, so I—" She couldn't hold back any longer, and threw her arms around him and Brian, who still clung, wide-eyed, to Mike.

"I have it all figured out," he said, not returning her hug, just barreling on, not giving her chance to say no. "I'll franchise the diner, so money won't be a problem. Maury and Barney will keep the restaurant going in the right direction under new management. Brian and I will move here—" he glanced around Suzy's tiny apartment "—and start looking for a larger place, maybe a house with a yard. You'll go to school, I'll take care of Brian and cook spectacular dinners for you. Every night you'll come home to us. That's all we want, whatever time you can give us."

He gazed at her pleadingly. Relief that the saddest

time of her life was coming to an end, plus a fierce and passionate love for both of them welled up in her heart. "I don't know," she said.

"Don't know what?" Now he looked desperate, but she hadn't fooled Brian. He was chortling and doing his best to clap his hands.

"Don't know if I like your plan."

His face fell. "No?"

"No. In the first place, you can't move in here. It's not my apartment. In the second place, you're not certain you want to franchise the diner. So what I was thinking…"

The way he was looking at her made her so sorry she'd hurt him that she hugged him tighter. Now that she was close enough, Brian took the opportunity to grab her hair and hang on to it as if it was a tree limb at the edge of Quechee Gorge.

They needed her, both of them, and depended on her. It was an effort not to burst into tears and throw herself at Mike's feet, begging for forgiveness. Instead, she forced herself to sound casual, as if the conversation hardly mattered to her at all.

"We'd stay in LaRocque, and you could stay with the diner whether you franchised it or not."

She felt the jolt that ran through him. "I found out I could arrange my classes so I'd only have to be here three days a week, and I'm sure Mom would take care of Brian while I'm gone. In fact, I think you'd have to hang her on a tree like a sap bucket to keep her from taking care of Brian." She guessed it was her turn to talk nonstop. "When you think the diner's under control enough for you to leave town, the two of you could be here with me, in a fairy-tale cottage with a picket fence or in an igloo. I don't care."

His face was so full of tentative hope that she felt that surge of love again. "Allie, are you saying..."

"Yes," she said crossly while snuggling her head into his shoulder, "I'm saying I was wrong. I'm saying that after I'm certified, I can't think of a place I'd rather set up a practice than in the valley. I'm saying—"

He cut her off with his kiss. With Brian's burbling sounds in their ears, they kissed as if they'd been apart for years and had just now discovered each other again.

Mike put Brian down on the floor and surrounded her with his strength and goodness and his love for her. If anybody could make it work, they could, because they couldn't make anything work without each other.

MIKE HAD a couple of questions on his mind, and as soon as he was able to let go of Allie, and as soon as they got Brian snuggled up for a nap, he decided he'd better address them before they went home to the furor of getting ready for the benefit the next night.

"Do you want another child?" he asked her, his mouth drifting over her ear.

He felt her delicious shiver. "As soon as I'm out of school, I'd love to have a baby with you."

"What about a linebacker-sized child, right now." He kissed her forehead and nuzzled her hair, and was startled when she leaped out of his arms.

"You want to adopt Maury," she said breathlessly. Her eyes were shining. "Oh, Mike, I was so hoping you would. He loves you so much. He already loves Brian, and Brian worships him. Oh, yes, yes, I would love to be Maury's mother. And Brian's. I'll adopt them both."

He pulled her back to him. "I'm Brian's brother

and his father," he whispered into her ear. "It will be complicated."

"We'll work it out. Right now, you're a daddy."

"And about to be a husband, I hope," he said, the idea setting off a wave of desire he'd act on as soon as he could. "One more thing," he said. "What shall we do about franchising the diner?"

She leaned back to look into his face. Those luscious brown eyes glowed at him, and a smile turned up the corners of her mouth. "Let's not," she said.

"Just what I wanted to hear," he said, and kissed her.

THE RECREATION room at the center glowed with candlelight and fall color. Dressed in their best, residents of the valley filled the tables to capacity. The sounds of their conversations and laughter filled the space with warmth and friendship.

Elaine was there, with her left hand extended. Allie smiled. Her mother had paid her back big-time. Her engagement to Barney, even the fact that they'd been seeing each other, had come as a total surprise.

"Planning to run away to Vegas?" Allie had asked, teasing her.

"Not this time, sweetheart. I've been thinking about Barney for three years."

Between dinner and dessert Daniel gave a short speech, thanking everyone for his or her support. Lilah spoke next, thanking the volunteers for their work. One by one, her committee heads came to the podium to thank their own volunteers.

It was Allie's turn. Glowing inside with happiness, she took the stage, thanking her people for flowers, plants and setting the tables. While she spoke, she scanned the room. It looked beautiful. The string quartet had only missed a few notes and broken one string. The meal had been—

Now was the glorious moment she would get to thank the most important people in her life. "Lilah, would you bring out the chefs?"

Lilah was already tugging Mike and Maury, both of them protesting, out of the kitchen. Allie observed that it was Maury who held Brian—exactly as Mike did, on his left hip.

They stood together on the dais, the four of them, while the audience gave them a standing ovation. Allie glanced at their faces. They knew. They knew they were looking at a family, and it hadn't even been a family until yesterday.

She shook her head. Ay-uh, as Barney would say, in a small town, news traveled fast.

* * * * *

Ian is the last single Foster brother left!
It'll take a special woman to get past his gruff
exterior... Be sure to find out who wins his heart in
Daly Thompson's next book,
DREAM DADDY,
available in May 2010!

Harlequin offers a romance for every mood!
See below for a sneak peek
from our paranormal romance line,
Silhouette® Nocturne™.
Enjoy a preview of REUNION by USA TODAY
bestselling author Lindsay McKenna.

Aella closed her eyes and sensed a distinct shift, like movement from the world around her to the unseen world.

She opened her eyes. And had a slight shock at the man standing ten feet away. He wasn't just any man. Her heart leaped and pounded. He reminded her of a fierce warrior from an ancient civilization. Incan? She wasn't sure but she felt his deep power and masculinity.

I'm Aella. Are you the guardian of this sacred site? she asked, hoping her telepathy was strong.

Fox's entire body soared with joy. Fox struggled to put his personal pleasure aside.

Greetings, Aella. I'm the assistant guardian to this sacred area. You may call me Fox. How can I be of service to you, Aella? he asked.

I'm searching for a green sphere. A legend says that the Emperor Pachacuti had seven emerald spheres created for the Emerald Key necklace. He had seven of his priestesses and priests travel the world to hide these spheres from evil forces. It is said that when all seven spheres are found, restrung and worn, that Light will return to the Earth. The fourth sphere is here, at your sacred site. Are you aware of it? Aella held her breath. She loved looking at him, especially his sensual mouth. The desire to kiss him came out of nowhere.

Fox was stunned by the request. *I know of the Emerald Key necklace because I served the emperor at the time it was created. However, I did not realize that one of the spheres is here.*

Aella felt sad. Why? Every time she looked at Fox, her heart felt as if it would tear out of her chest. *May I stay in touch with you as I work with this site?* she asked.

Of course. Fox wanted nothing more than to be here with her. To absorb her ephemeral beauty and hear her speak once more.

Aella's spirit lifted. What *was* this strange connection between them? Her curiosity was strong, but she had more pressing matters. In the next few days, Aella knew her life would change forever. How, she had no idea....

Look for REUNION
by USA TODAY *bestselling author*
Lindsay McKenna,
available April 2010, only from
Silhouette® Nocturne™.

HARLEQUIN® Romance®

**ROMANCE, RIVALRY
AND A FAMILY REUNITED**

THE BRIDES
of
BELLA ROSA

William Valentine and his beloved wife, Lucia, live
a beautiful life together, but when his former love Rosa
and the secret family they had together resurface,
an instant rivalry is formed. Can these families
get through the past and come together as one?

*Step into the world of Bella Rosa
beginning this April with*

Beauty and the Reclusive Prince
by
RAYE MORGAN

Eight volumes to collect and treasure!

www.eHarlequin.com

HRI7650

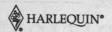

HARLEQUIN®
INTRIGUE®

WILL THIS REUNITED FAMILY
BE STRONG ENOUGH TO EXPOSE
A LURKING KILLER?

FIND OUT IN THIS ALL-NEW
THRILLING TRILOGY FROM TOP
HARLEQUIN INTRIGUE AUTHOR

B.J. DANIELS

WHITEHORSE
MONTANA

Winchester Ranch

GUN-SHY BRIDE—*April 2010*

HITCHED—*May 2010*

TWELVE-GAUGE GUARDIAN—
June 2010

HI69465

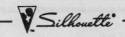